Writer's Cramp

About the Author

Alan Blackwood was a publishing editor for many years, before he moved to the other side of the desk as the author of numerous books and other features on music. Most recently still, he has turned to fiction. A number of his very short stories (flash fiction) have already appeared in print, and a collection of these pieces is being prepared for publication. *Writer's Cramp* is his first full-length work.

Alan Blackwood

Writer's Cramp

Olympia Publishers
London

www.olympiapublishers.com
OLYMPIA PAPERBACK EDITION

A CIP catalogue record for this title is
available from the British Library.

ISBN: 978-1-84897-687-0

(Olympia Publishers is part of Ashwell Publishing Ltd)

First published in 2016

Olympia Publishers
60 Cannon Street
London
EC4N 6NP

Printed in Great Britain

'Christ, just look at it!' Iris said. It was one of those days when the longer it rained the harder it rained. A spout of water from a faulty gutter hit the deck with a smackety smack, like the slapping of fat buttocks. In the echoing well of the building the office lights were on. Come rain or shine, they always were, illuminating the occupants like goldfish in a bowl. Catch them picking their noses.

I dumped the typescript on her desk, with my brief report tucked under the elastic band.

'Any good?' Iris asked absently.

'It's got one or two good points,' I said of the novel in question, 'but it's rather heavy going.'

Let's be honest, it was ponderous, hackneyed, and it didn't stand a chance. The many corrections and deletions on the page simply made things worse. It was also somebody's baby, probably as precious to them as a creature of flesh and blood. There were plenty of people who claimed they could write a book, or boasted that they were going to. How many of them ever put pen to paper. How many tried and staggered on for a bit before they called it a day. That left the real heroes who struggled doggedly through to the end, keeping faith with themselves through the weeks, the months, maybe years of private and solitary labour. This poor sod for one, and though his labour of love might have been in vain, the fact that he'd finished it at all was a huge achievement. He deserved a medal.

That said, there was no time for sentiment. There were others out there who'd also made it to the end, and their stuff came in each day by the sackful. It was called the slush pile, all those unsolicited manuscripts, and it was a cruel and a merciless place. Perhaps as few as one in twenty of them were considered to show any promise at all, and maybe only one in a hundred of those ever got accepted.

Iris glanced at my report and flipped casually through a couple of pages of the dog-eared typescript. It had been round the houses.

'I don't know,' she said, 'how you can go on, day after day, reading all this crap. You must get punch drunk.'

Yes. And I reckoned I was getting to the point where I couldn't tell good from bad. Publisher's reader sounded impressive, but I'd rot if I didn't move on soon. And come to think of it, what right had I to sit in judgement over other people's work when I'd done nothing myself.

Iris's phone always made me jump. She grabbed it. 'Yes! Oh, for God's sake, Giles!'

She sat back, receiver to her ear, with that weak and exasperated look she sometimes put on. She put a hand over the mouthpiece. 'You dropped something,' she said to me.

I picked up the envelope, waved a hand, and left.

*

It was the weekly letter from mum. Her writing spun limply across the page like wool drawn from a ball. What made me think of that? Why knitting, of course. It was the one thing she enjoyed and was any real good at. See and hear them, as I did as a toddler, at the Women's Fellowship knitting circle in the church hall up by the allotments, fingers twitching and tugging at the wool as a spider tests the threads of its web, needles clicking frantically like the call of insects on heat, embryonic socks dangling like woolly condoms. A lot of Freudian transference going on by the sound and the look of it. And afterwards the choruses of 'I Will Make You Fishers Of Men' and 'Count Your Blessings One By One,' sung with such passion to the rhubarb and the runner beans. The tea urn and the clatter of cups, the furtive farts, it's a wonder the vicar could stand it.

*

A Fisher of Men? My mum? I never even saw her hold hands with my dad. Much too demonstrative, much too everything. For both of them. How they hell they ever had me is one of the great mysteries of the universe. If there was a word beyond impossible I'd use it. Perhaps I was a changeling, or I'd sprung from the loins of an incubus. That might explain what went on in my infant mind, the abominable acts and images that crowded into it, enough to make any half decent shrink reach for the smelling salts or bring a blush to the cheeks of the Maquis de Sade. Of course, it might be that we all think and imagine the same sorts of things and just keep very quiet about it. Otherwise, dumped in a corner of the church hall with a picture book and a glass of lemonade, it's a good job there wasn't any holy water around. One drop on me and I'd have gone up in flames.

*

'Give my love to Ann'. Mum always ended her letters with that little mantra. Say it or write it enough times and everything would be all right. It had to be. Getting married at the altar and in the presence of God, then divorced, didn't happen in her world. Nor did the trauma of falling in love, the huge emotional eruption, then getting chewed up and spat out again. A propos of that, consider all the poetry and song, from the most elevated and inspired to the most weary and banal, in praise of such a madness. And why that huge excess of feeling, why such an emotional overkill, when all that nature required was a good honest bonk.

I crumpled up mum's letter and tossed it into the wastepaper basket. My office, for want of a better name, might have been a linen cupboard or slops room when the building was a block of service flats. Large pipes ran round the skirting, so that I couldn't stand my metal table against the wall. It wobbled each time I hammered away at Tiger Tank, my ancient typewriter that weighed a ton. There was also my chair, of the kind you used to see in doctors' waiting rooms, an angle-poise lamp that didn't poise much anymore, and that wastepaper basket, also made of some green-painted metal and which I suppose should therefore be called a bin. At least I couldn't see the rain through the frosted glass.

*

It trickled down the station steps, and down onto the platform. It dripped from the little stalactites (unless they were stalagmites) that hung from the sooty tunnel entrance, on the oldest stretch of underground railway in the world, from Baker Street to Farringdon Road. There was a photograph of Mr Gladstone, in stovepipe hat, emerging from one of the tunnels in a truck, perhaps that very one.

Some drips fell upon the live conductor rail. I thought that water and electricity could be pretty lethal, like electrocuting yourself in the bath. A train came in on the opposite platform. Wait for it to start again and watch what happened when the conducting shoe from the motor made contact with the live wet rail. Yes, there was a flash, a splutter and a moment's loss of traction. But don't wait for the driver and his passengers to light up like beacons with their hair in flames.

Pissing onto the live rail might be a more promising scenario. Hurled back against the station wall with five hundred volts up your blackened dick. Certainly a more inventive way to go than throwing yourself in front of the train, with all the mess and inconvenience. Of course it might not always be a straight case of suicide but the terrible attraction of the platform edge and the desire to experience the moment of no return as you stepped off it, much like jumping off a cliff. I sometimes had dreams of doing the one or the other and waking at the moment I fell. And would I die if I didn't wake up?

My train came in and nobody jumped, though it may have crossed their mind. The carriage seemed more packed than usual, with all those damp and swollen clothes and dripping umbrellas, beginning to dry and to exude a smell of stale potato peelings. People stared at folded newspapers, not reading them, just pretending they weren't there. Change at King's Cross, down the escalator and deeper into the saturated clay, where the tunnels turned and twisted, like copulating worms.

*

'Ah, there you are young man!' Hugh exclaimed. He must be a few years older than me, but soon enough I'd look older than him, if I didn't already. Hugh was a mannequin, smooth waxy face, hair pulled back over his scalp and not a shred of it out of place, pinstripe suit, spotted tie (white spots on blue), black laced shoes and, would you believe it, suspenders attached to those long grey woollen socks. He still lived at home, and while my landlady gave me a greasy fried egg for breakfast I'll bet his mother gave him a soft boiled one with little slices of buttered toast.

Hugh's desk was as spotless and virginal as the rest of him. There was a snow-white blotting pad, a desk calendar, a pencil sharpener and three freshly sharpened pencils of exactly the same length lined up beside the pad. There was also, at that moment, the cover artwork for *Dead Dames Tell No Tales*, the title spelt out in letters of blood above the face of a pulchritudinous blonde with lots of teeth and lipstick and emitting a silent scream.

'The usual run down.' Hugh polished his horn-rimmed glasses, inspected them at arm's length, and handed me the typescript of another book, *Inspector Flint and the Mayfair Murders*. Hugh's typescripts had to be as immaculate as everything else about him, and if they didn't come like that from the author he had them retyped, deducting the cost from what were euphemistically called royalties. That is, from the advance, since the sale of Hugh's books, hardback, paperback, book club editions, could be reckoned down to the last five copies, and the royalties on those sales were nicely calculated never to exceed the advance. So there they were, his stable of authors, each contracted to deliver three titles a year, not less than seventy thousand, not more than seventy five thousand words. The giddy cocktail of the crime-writer's life.

The thing about Hugh's typescripts was that you could make a pretty good guess at the word count just by looking at them. I'd say seventy three thousand for this one. Let's have a look inside. Page one:

'The phone rang just as Inspector Flint was reaching for his hat. "It's for you, sir," said Sergeant Bruce, handing him the instrument. "Flint," he barked into it.'

Last page: 'Sergeant Bruce looked puzzled as he took the wheel. "There's still one thing I don't understand, sir," he said.'

Think of the author, sitting in his little upstairs study, looking out onto a small back garden, with the rattle of a train at the end of it, busting a gut over every hackneyed word.

'Well up to standard,' I typed. Tiger Tank's keys hit the paper like gunshots. His letter 'o' cut small circles into it. Bullet holes for Hugh.

*

The artwork for another book cover now lay on Iris's cluttered desk. The words *Dark Destiny* were scrawled in letters not of blood but of flame across a man and a woman in vaguely Regency attire, locked in an embrace. Enough to make Inspector Flint throw up.

'Got a moment?' I asked.

Iris looked up from whatever typescript she was nervously picking at with her pencil. 'Make it quick.'

'You know you said how I must get punch drunk, reading all this crap.'

'Did I?'

'Yes. And you also said you could do with some editorial assistance.'

Iris dropped her pencil, sat back and sighed. 'You can say that again!'

'Well, perhaps you could send a memo to the boss recommending me.'

There was a tap tap on her door. 'Who is it?' Another tap. Iris raised her voice. 'I said, who is it? Come in!'

A tall man, with sandy hair and in need of a shave, poked his head round the door, hesitated when he saw me, then entered sideways.

'For Christ's sake, Giles!' Iris picked up her pencil again as though to stab someone with it. 'I told you never to come up here!'

He produced a large handkerchief from a pocket of his shabby green corduroy suit and noisily blew his nose. 'I was just round this way and - '

'Shut the door, shut the door!'

Giles stuffed the hankie back in his pocket. 'Any chance of a cup of tea?'

'No!'

'So that's arranged then,' I said.

Iris swung her head round from Giles back to me. 'What? Oh, yes, yes!'

*

Oh, no, no. And thank God. If I'd got embroiled with *Dark Destiny* I'd probably not have seen that modest little notice tucked away among the small ads in *The Bookseller* about an editorial job working with a new edition of *The Universal Book of Knowledge*. The man in charge was Mr Bird, and his toothbrush moustache was more Charlie Chaplin than Adolf Hitler. He rested his arms on top of his desk, clasped his hands together and cleared his throat. 'I think you might fit in,' he said.

I did, into the cubby hole that was even smaller than the one I'd left behind. No problem there. If you're happy in what you're doing nothing much else matters. I had a pile of layout sheets, a glue pot, a pair of scissors, a red pencil and a blue one. The real stuff of publishing at last, the sharp end. First job, updating the maps. Couldn't have suited me better.

Maps and atlases had always been some sort of escape for me. I used to stand on the beach (a ten minute bus ride from home) and wonder what lay over the sea's horizon. France, of course. But what were things like over there and everywhere else beyond our shores? Was the grass blue and the sky green abroad, and what was it like to breathe the air, unless it was something like helium?

Let the atlases and the maps carry me from Calais all the way across Russia and Siberia to Vladivostok; from Cairo down the Nile into darkest Africa; from Maine, over the Appalachians, across the prairies and the Rockies to the far shores of the Pacific; or down the spine of the Andes to what looked like the coccyx of Tierra del Fuego, volcanoes and snow and the Roaring Forties.

Speaking of things anatomical, there was the foot of Italy kicking at Sicily; the scrawny fingers of the Peloponnese reaching for the island of Crete; Kintyre dangling off the west coast of Scotland like a donkey's prick; Florida, below the paunch of Georgia, dripping its island keys into the Gulf of Mexico; Korea, a diseased appendix attached to China; New Guinea, a plesiosaur cresting the waves of some primordial sea. And away from anatomy or whatever, look at the state of Nevada, the blade of a guillotine.

Everywhere on the map as familiar to me as the back of my hand. The reality must be a very different matter. What if I was suddenly transported to the Tibesti Mountains in the middle of the Sahara, the air shuddering with a heat to pop out my eyeballs and scorch my lungs. Or the North Cape in winter, the sea freezing over, while the night sky flickered eerily with the lights of the aurora borealis, where the solar wind met the Earth's magnetic field.

*

I tapped on Mr Bird's door. He jerked his head up and adjusted his glasses. It was after lunch.

'Livorno,' I said to him. 'We don't want to call it Leghorn any more do we?'

He cleared his throat once more while he cleared his mind. 'Leghorn?'

'The port in Italy.'

'Ah yes. No, you're right. Livorno, I think.'

'What about Naples?'

'What about it?'

'Napoli?'

'Oh no,' Mr Bird's voice sank. 'I think that's going a bit too far.' He cleared his throat yet again and leaned forward over his desk. 'By the way we may be moving soon. I hope you'll be coming with us.'

In expectation, a pigeon took off from his window sill. The building was encrusted with pigeon shit, like mouldy icing on a wedding cake. One day the weight of it might send us sliding into the Farringdon Road and down to the river Fleet. The flush of a toilet somewhere in the building signalled that something was already on its way.

*

Gazing again at my maps, I took in some of those political boundaries. What stories did they tell of war, violence and chicanery or of pure muddle and accident. It was impossible to see the point in some of them. There was Afghanistan poking a crooked finger deep into the Hindu Kush. Who had scrambled up those arid mountains to map that out, and why? Who had decided the border between Quebec Province and Labrador? Some half-drunk fur trapper with theodolite and compass, and his Eskimo guide, lurching through the snowy forests and over the icy rivers and lakes, to plot that squiggly line. And what crazy Spanish conquistador hacked his way through the Amazonian rain forests, in defiance of all the snakes and spiders and tropical diseases, just to say which parts of it belonged to Peru, Bolivia, Venezuela and Brazil?

'Livorno' I wrote importantly with my blue pencil, and paused to scan mum's latest letter. Sometimes she had a nugget of news. The Reverend Guinness had passed away. 'You'll remember him,' she wrote.

I certainly did. At Women's Fellowship they called him the Reverend Guin*ness* to distance him from the famous brew, though standing tall in black cassock and white dog collar he looked quite like a pint of it. He used to ride around his cosy suburban parish, about as far removed from events in Roman Palestine two thousand years ago as it was possible to imagine, calling on his flock. One day he caught my dad at home. God has a Message for all of us, he said, standing there in his bicycle clips, with a cup of tea in one hand and the other raised hopefully aloft, while my dad crouched in his armchair, grinning like a man with a noose around his neck.

Next time I saw him he sat there still, in the same old armchair, threads of it hanging loose where the cat exercised her claws. And the noose had tightened with the years.

'Could do with a spot of rain, old man,' he said to me breathlessly. He always said that. My dad didn't believe in too much sun and dry weather and warmth. It might turn you soft and into a bit of a pansy. Rain and an edge to the wind, a patch of mud to fall into, a wash in cold water, making snowballs with your bare hands, that's what built you up. Now, of course, a touch of heat aggravated his emphysema. Before that got too bad he'd busied himself in retirement with his carpentry, making chess tables that nobody could use, and a small wooden figure attached by its arms to a kind of weathervane on top of the bird table, that bobbed up and down with the wind. Right now it pumped away, poor little wanker, as the rising wind brought spongy grey clouds racing over the rooftops.

Dad was going to get his rain, by the looks of it. And lunch in the front room, since it was a Sunday and I was a kind of guest these days. Mum's gravy left its mark round the plate like one of the rings of Saturn, the pastry was flabby, the custard full of lumps.

'Eat up, old man,' my dad said. He'd been doing it for over forty years.

*

Mr Bird blinked as sunlight glanced off the steel and glass facade of Galaxy House. The move he'd spoken of had come about and we were joining the parent company in their state-of-the-arts new premises.

'My word,' he said, wiping the sweat band of his pork-pie hat. 'We are going up in the world!'

There came a sudden roar from somewhere. 'What's that!' he cried with some alarm. An airliner climbed above the trees, tipped a silver wing and headed for the clouds, trailing smoke.

'Heathrow,' I said and nearly gagged. Here was the madness of love and its aftermath. Heathrow was where she - whose name I could hardly bear to recall let alone speak out loud - worked, and not too far from where she lived, and within a circumference of about ten miles it was all an emotionally toxic fall-out zone. I couldn't go near it. And yet God help me, there I was. I couldn't have been listening when Mr Bird told me where we were moving to.

I might have bolted on the spot. Instead I sat at a smart new desk in the smart new open-plan office on the eleventh floor of Galaxy House, waiting for Mr Bird to tell me what to do next and aimlessly shifting my maps around. My desk was by the windows, and from them I looked down on a scruffy row of shops, a boarded-up church by the dried-out duck pond, and the road that crossed the railway tracks by the oil storage tanks and vanished somewhere among the cabbage fields and pig farms, beyond which tail planes manoeuvred like sharks around the airport buildings. She worked shift hours. At any time she might be there.

Turn the other way and there was Daphne (I think that was her name). Pudding basin haircut, fat red face, eyes screwed up against the smoke from the fag in her mouth, boobs and thighs testing to breaking point the tensile strength of her tweeds, while she hammered away at a typewriter and shot glances at nubile types by the drinks dispenser. She never looked at me, thank God.

*

As for Mr Bird, I never knew what happened to him, but his words about going up in the world came back to me as I pressed the button by the front door of the tall Georgian terraced house. There was a Greek restaurant in the basement. Then, according to the smudgy names against the other buttons, a dry cleaners, a travel firm and a dating agency. Top of the list was Omega Books. I pressed the button a second time and waited.

From afar there came the sound of someone hurtling down some wooden stairs, probably two at a time. The source of this frantic activity flung open the front door. 'Entry phone's on the blink,' he panted, leading the way rather more slowly back up however many flights of stairs it was.

'Take a seat.' We both got our breath back. His office ceiling followed the slope of the roof with one small window set into it. On his desk was a framed photograph, and a fancy letter opener fashioned into a miniature claymore. Otherwise the room was pretty spartan. He jabbed with the claymore at my letter of application.

'Universal Book of Knowledge,' he repeated quickly. Thin and pale in his dark suit and white shirt with a very tight knot in his tie, he looked as though he was strung with piano wires tuned to concert pitch. 'What was all that about?'

'I think I said it was an encyclopaedia.'

'No, no, why did you leave?'

'I was made redundant.'

'On what grounds?'

'They stopped work on it. I think it was what they call a company tax loss, or something of the sort.'

My prospective employer sniffed, nodded and fingered his claymore.

'So was Omega Books. But that's all changed. My brief now is to bring the imprint back into profit.' He spoke fast, and as though someone kept prodding him with that damned claymore. 'Omega Books used to occupy nearly the whole of this building, and they were leaders in their field. We will be again. My first job is to recruit a dedicated team. Think you're up to it?'

He brushed back a long, limp lock of fair hair. 'You've studied our backlist, of course.'

Somewhere close by and down below was a wing of the British Museum. The Egyptian Gallery perhaps. Sarcophagi and mummies and all that sort of thing. I had an idea there was a connection.

'Well, yes.'

'You're interested in the occult?'

'Well, I -'

'What's your sun sign?'

'My sign?'

'When's your birthday?'

'I thought I said I was - '

'No, no. Your day and month of birth.'

I told him.

'Really!' Adrian sat back and nibbled at a fingernail.

*

Maybe that's what got me the job, being on the cusp, as I think Adrian called it. At any rate astrology seemed to have come to my rescue.

Cindy, on the other hand, was a great gust of fresh air. 'Jeez, look at that then!' Hollow-eyed faces stared back at us from a picture of crepuscular gloom.

'It's a spirit painting by - .' I peered closer at the page. 'Looks like Austin Osman Spare.'

'I'll go spare in a minute!'

Cindy was a big girl with rosy cheeks, a fuzzy Afro hairdo, and orange plastic earrings. A few years on and she'd make a lovely pearly queen. Not Adrian's type at all, I'd have thought, but with an agency you couldn't pick and choose.

'*The Secrets of the Grimoyers,*' she read on the cover of another volume, which carried the image of a pentacle inside a circle, with a lot of weird signs and symbols.

'*Grimoires*, I think, Cindy.'

'What was they, then?'

'Search me.'

'Well, how do you know how I should say it?'

'Looks French, that's all.'

She thumbed through an old Omega catalogue. 'Blimey, there's an advert in 'ere for crystal balls!' There was too.

We shared the room next to Adrian's, with another window set into the sloping roof. The room opposite was a charnel house of more ancient books and manuscripts, bundles of correspondence and contracts, preserved in dust as black as pepper. You could choke to death in there. It got hot and stuffy enough in our room most days now that summer had arrived.

'Phew!' Cindy propped open the sash window with one fat volume. *Foundations of Tibetan Mysticism.* 'Let's 'ave another.' She reached for *The Egyptian Book of the Dead.*

Adrian froze in horror at the door. 'What the hell d'you think you're doing!'

Cindy clapped the dust off her hands. 'We gotta breathe, ain't we?'

'But they're file copies. They're irreplaceable.'

'All right, you find somethin' then.' We jammed in an old wooden ruler where the sash cord used to be.

'Eugh!' She'd found what claimed to be the photograph of a man sitting slumped in a chair with what looked like cobwebs coming out of his mouth, down his nose and from his ears. 'Wot's goin' on 'ere?'

Adrian grabbed the book and stared at the picture, one eye opened wider than the other.

'Ectoplasm,' he pronounced. 'Mediums produce it while they're in a trance. Spirits are supposed to materialise inside it.'

'Oo-er!' Cindy cried, fanning herself with the catalogue advertising crystal balls.

*

One day I must take her round to that joke shop right across the road from the British Museum and we'd have a good old giggle at those huge rubbery hairy hands, giant black spiders dangling on a spring, or one of those model turds, of an amazing verisimilitude, called a Dirty Fido or a Mucky Pup. Who the hell made them and what did they put on their passport?

Come to think of it, I'd never seen anyone in that shop. It was the same with those premises that sold things called trusses and belts and other strange, deeply private and deeply puzzling medical impedimenta. Was our joke shop a front for drugs or sex trafficking and prostitution, or maybe a cover for MI5? Password, Mucky Pup.

Oomph! We collided at the corner of the street. Handbag, permanent wave, prim little dab of lipstick, and a pixie sexiness poking through.

'Iris!'

'Good Lord!' She patted down her coat. 'What are you doing round here?'

'I work just up the road.'

'Weren't you on some encyclopaedia thing?'

'Not any more. Omega Books, if you've heard of them.'

'Don't they publish all that mumbo jumbo stuff?'

'If that's what you want to call it. By the way, how's *Dark Destiny* doing?'

'What?'

'The last time I was in your office you had the cover artwork on your desk.'

'Did I?'

'Best seller?'

'Don't be funny. I've finished with Giles, by the way.'

'Giles?'

'Come on, you remember.'

'Big tall chap, corduroys, sandy hair, kept blowing his nose?'

'Yes!'

'Boy friend?'

'My husband, for God's sake!'

A dishevelled oaf like that. He might not always have been, of course.

'Oh,' Iris added, 'and I've moved. House, that is. Look, come round soon and meet Sam. My lodger. He's adorable, and bloody good in bed.' She fished out a card. 'Ring me. Must dash.'

Must dash. I'm sure she didn't have to. She just did. Anything to stop facing up to herself, I'd say. Not just her, the whole bloody world, running away from itself all the time. Well, not me, not for a little while. I lay back on my mattress on the floor of my new pad and, I suddenly realised, truly on my own for the first time in my life. It was like feeling the mind or spirit give a great big yawn.

In my peace and solitude I was also aware as never before of the objects round about me, the door, the kitchen table, my coffee mug with the yellow smiling face. They took on identities of their own, and they were waiting for something. Left undisturbed they might wait for a thousand, ten thousand years. Time meant nothing. I gazed up at the ceiling where the plaster formed hundreds of little whorls like craters on the moon, each casting a tiny shadow from the naked light bulb hanging by its flex. Funny how that glowing bulb suddenly seemed such a long, long way away, a hundred, a thousand, a hundred million miles, shining like Jupiter. And the window, absolutely enormous, as though I was seeing it from a mile off.

Ten minutes of meditation, if you could call it that, and I was beginning to hallucinate. No wonder those prophets and saints and holy men, half-starved and living alone in a cave in the middle of the desert for fifty years, saw visions and heard voices. Was it Saint Anthony who was pictured in all those old prints, etchings and woodcuts surrounded in his delirium by hideous demons, the kind of thing you might experience on a very bad trip? The Temptation of Saint Anthony, that's what those images were called. And what temptations would they have been? Carnal ones? I wouldn't have thought so. After fifty years stuck out in his cave he'd hardly have remembered what a woman looked like, and living on bread and water or whatever I'm sure he wouldn't have cared.

An aircraft passed across my window, navigation lights winking red and white in the thickening dusk, the passengers tired, cramped and stiff, impatient to land and get through Heathrow as quickly as they could. Just a name to them.

*

'You can kill that.' Kenneth dropped the manuscript of *The Search for the Holy Grail* on my desk. Another one from our rather more recondite slush pile. His report, for want of a better word, would have made Hugh's suspenders twang. It was scribbled on the back of a used envelope. 'Absolute balls,' it read. 'On no account publish.'

Kenneth was tall and gaunt with a dab of cotton wool on his face where he'd nicked himself with the razor. He wore a crumpled pinstripe suit and a dusty black homburg hat, and carried around an old brown patent leather case. The back street abortionist of old. What set him apart was the pipe. There was a strip of plaster round the stem and the bowl was burnt down one side like the lip of a volcano. He put a match to it with no observable result.

'Anything else?' he asked me.

'This just came in.'

Kenneth shunted the typescript round. *Know Your Aura* by Sylvia Bloom. He snatched the pipe from his mouth. 'Yah, yah, yah, yah, yah!' Now there was a guffaw, along with a quantity of dribble.

'You know her?' I asked.

'Know her stuff.'

So did I, up to a point. I was getting familiar with our backlist, in which Sylvia Bloom loomed large. *The Opening of the Third Eye*, *The Road to Spiritual Healing*, *Voices from the Other Side*, all with rave reviews in *The Psychic News*.

'What's it like?'

'Woolly-minded nonsense.' Kenneth dumped *Know Your Aura* into his case. 'Where's the other chap?'

'Adrian. He's not in today. Got a migraine.'

'Well tell him I'm off to the country for a few weeks. The Castle, Wallingford, if he needs me.'

Did he say Wallingford, my Wallingford? I was back as a child in Paddington Station, then still wreathed in smoke and steam, a glass and iron womb that sent me down the gleaming steel tracks, crossing, multiplying, dividing, to the final stretch of branch line, the umbilical cord that delivered me to that place of gas lamps and shadows, river and cloud. The walk over the bridge, across the water meadows and down the avenue of horse chestnut trees to the abandoned chapel, little gothic tower half strangled in the clutch of ivy, tombs and headstones sinking back into black earth, twilit nave with fallen timbers and plaster across pews and flagstones, fingers of creeper poking through broken lattice window panes, and the silence of eternity. Or the path through the Castle grounds, guided by stone walls and banks of nettles, that descended in deep shade past the high mound of the Keep, entered a short tunnel and came out again by the town cemetery, where the air was dark with the call of rooks.

'I used to go to Wallingford on school holidays.'

'Good Lord.' Kenneth grabbed his case. 'Small world.' The reek of his pipe hung in the stuffy room.

'Who's that then?' For once Cindy was quite subdued.

'Kenneth Brewster, our literary adviser.'

'Bit of a card, ain't 'e?'

'A touch of the aristocracy there, I shouldn't wonder.'

'Nevah!' she whispered hoarsely.

*

Cindy was a wonderful gust of fresh air, lifting the fog, the miasma, that had settled on me for far too long. The landscape broadened, and I wanted to belong again. Our Playmates singles club for a start. We weren't spring chickens, any of us, and we'd all been through the mill one way or another and come out the other side. Mind you, there were probably plenty of others who'd love to join a singles club and knock around a bit more if only they had the chance. The grass is always greener, as they say.

Saturday was our big night of the week, when we jumped into our cars (even I now had a little one of those) and took another spin at the wheel, round the circuit of amber-lit dual carriageways, the shopping malls and industrial estates, through a hundred sets of lights, till we dropped with a bounce and a tinkle into that night's slot. See us come through the front door clutching our bottle with a smile of expectancy changed to the rictus of a grin by the time we reached the kitchen. The same old bunch of losers. Still, chin up.

'That looks interesting.' Not always the same old bunch either. The female in question indicated the bottle I'd just added to the motley collection by the kitchen sink, wet with some of their contents.

'You think so?'

'Well, no.' She kind of chuckled and fluttered her eyelashes. 'My name's Penny, by the way.'

I waved a hand round the kitchen. 'This is a bit different from the usual.' Indeed it looked like the biggest room I'd ever been in, with one of those boxes of discs that opened and closed for room service above the door. One disc was stuck half way in a sly wink. Come up and see me some time.

'I suppose it is quite grand.' Penny was no spring chicken either, with those little crows' feet at the corner of her eyes, one or two grey hairs among the brown, but not old, sort of ageless, like Hugh, though that was where any resemblance ended. There was a happy carelessness about her dress and the casual dab of lipstick.

I asked, 'Are you a new member?'

Penny shook her head. 'I shouldn't really be here at all.'

'Why not?'

'I came along with a friend who's a friend of the lady of the house.'

'Is she around?'

'I think she's in China at the moment.'

Now I remembered, it was the housekeeper who'd laid the party on.

Penny accepted a drop of my plonk and looked at me coyly over the rim of her glass. 'May I ask what you do?'

'I'm in publishing.'

'I knew it would be something interesting!' A bit of a tease as well. 'Do tell me what you publish.'

'Occult books.'

'Gosh!' There was a word you didn't hear much anymore, at least not in my circles. Penny rummaged about in the hand-knitted bag that hung from her arm. 'I mean, this really is a coincidence. May I take your phone number?' She blushed deeply. 'Your office number, I mean. I might like to get in touch.'

'About something you've written?'

'Not me. I'm not clever enough. Somebody else.'

She scribbled down the number and dropped pencil and paper back in her bag. She followed my gaze. 'What are you looking at?'

'That chap. I think he's got a glass eye.'

'Yes,' Penny agreed. 'It's like wigs. You can always tell.'

'I knew someone with a glass eye when I was in digs. My landlady's old man. It wasn't a great big china orb, like they use in waxworks, couldn't be when you come to think about it, trying to get something like that in and out of the socket. Quite small really, kind of saucer shaped. He used to clean it at breakfast time then slip it back under the empty socket so that half of his face looked frozen as though he'd had a stroke, then try and sip his tea out of a saucer.'

There came a sudden thump of decibels from another room. 'Like to dance?'

Penny tried shouting back but her voice, soft and kittenish, wasn't made for it. I think it was something about looking for her friend. At the kitchen door, beneath the box of tricks, she turned and waved with the tips of her fingers and sank into the crowd.

*

'Glass eyes are funny things, aren't they Cindy,' I said, with Penny still on my mind. 'You can't blink with a glass eye.'

'Fishes and snakes don't blink, neither.' Cindy blew on her freshly painted 'sassy pink' nails. 'Who's he got in there then?' She nodded towards Adrian's room.

We soon found out. He stuck his head round our door and beckoned to me. 'Come in a minute, will you.'

Daphne sat in his visitor's chair. She was tarted up a bit, but there was little or nothing she could do about the boobs, the fat lips, the boiled beetroot look.

Adrian said, 'I'd like you to meet Sylvia Bloom.'

She waved away the smoke from her cigarette and, like a fish or a snake, didn't bat an eyelid. Nor did I, come to that.

Adrian asked me, 'Has Brewster's report come in yet?'

'Brewster?' Sylvia Bloom (as I'd better start calling her) sat up sharply. It was the first time I'd heard her speak. 'Kenneth Brewster?' she snapped huskily.

Adrian sat back in his chair looking pleased with himself. 'Yes, top man in his field.'

Sylvia stubbed out her cigarette in the wastepaper basket. 'Isn't he into black magic?'

For a moment I could think only of chocolates, and Adrian shot forward, the front legs of his chair hitting the floor.

Sylvia casually lit another cigarette. 'Diabolism, necromancy, that sort of thing.'

For once Adrian was lost for words. He reached for his claymore and looked helplessly at me. 'Er, could we have some coffee.'

Cindy plugged in the kettle. 'What's she like then?'

'You wouldn't believe it but I've met her before, under a different name. I shared an office with her for a few days, in my last job. Big, busty and butch. Well, more than a bit, I'd say.'

'Strewth!' Cindy dipped a spoon in the powdered milk.

'Black for her, and no sugar.'

'Bloody hell!'

'Keep your voice down.'

I had Kenneth's report on *Know Your Aura* on my desk and it could stay there till Sylvia had gone.

*

A skip loaded with rotten timbers, a lot of old plumbing and a lavatory seat, upon which perched a headless garden gnome, stood in a pool of stagnant water outside the new address Iris had given me, in a street of Victorian terraced houses.

She came to the front door in slacks and blouse. 'Three weeks I've been waiting for them to remove that thing.' She slammed the door shut behind me. 'Three weeks!' She led the way down the short corridor. 'We'll have to eat in the kitchen.'

Somebody else was in there, very tall for what might be his age, fair skinned and sandy haired.

'You haven't met Clifford, have you?'

Clifford shot out a hand and withdrew it again before I'd had a chance to shake it. Iris put on a glove and opened the oven to a sauna-like blast of heat.

'God almighty, Clifford! I told you to keep an eye on the joint.'

'Sorry mum.'

'Well, where's the wine?'

He lunged at the refrigerator door.

'Not red wine in the fridge, Clifford!'

'Sorry mum.'

'No problem.' I handed over my bottle. 'We can start with mine.'

Iris stepped into the hall. 'Sam!'

A small dark man of Levantine aspect, with the makings of a five o clock shadow, came slowly down the stairs combing his hair. He joined us and made a hash of carving what was left of the joint.

I asked the assembled company, 'Is that a grand piano in the other room?'

It was Sam who brightened. 'Do you play?'

'I had lessons as a child.'

From a dear old gentleman with a soft pink face and voice to match, who exuded a smell of something like camphor that went perfectly with the spats and stiff winged collar. If he'd been tougher with me maybe I'd have learnt more. It certainly wasn't fear that marked my heavy tread after school on Friday afternoons, the week's slog not yet over, back to that gloomy street of large grey houses, walls streaked an aspidistra green from faulty guttering, the other face of Brighton, over the hill and away from the sea. It was guilt - another week and no more practice done. The music was there inside me but shackled by the tyranny of those maddening little dots on the stave lines, EGBDF (Every Good Boy Deserves Fun) in the treble clef. I'm sure I'd have got round to it all, the notes, the keys and scales, the crotchets and quavers, if I'd also been allowed to seek out some of those chords, have a bash at some of those rhythms, ringing in my head. I just couldn't do things by the book. And I certainly didn't deserve those sticky buns.

'Can you read chord signs?' Sam asked.

If by chord signs he meant such things as C7-9, Gm6, then I'd sometimes seen them on sheet music, like some arcane and fascinating code for snatching harmonies out of thin air. Something I'm sure my old teacher would have viewed with horror.

'I'll show you in a minute,' Sam said.

Iris glanced at the kitchen clock. 'You want to hear the Schubert, don't you sweetie?'

'Yes mum.'

In the living room the paper was stripped from the walls and everything was under sheets. Through the French windows a swing with a broken seat stood amidst the knee-high grass and

33

weeds. Iris removed the sheets from some chairs and from a venerable radiogram. Schubert's C Major Quintet commenced and somewhere a dog began to bark.

'Christ!' Iris cried. 'If that bloody animal craps on my path one more time I'm calling the police!'

Poor Schubert, Dirty Fido.

*

We didn't keep pets in Linden Court and there was a no smoking sign in the entrance hall. We didn't live in each other's pockets either. We bustled off to work, came home again, nodded to each other in passing, and retired, each to his or her own private vault.

'What've you got there then?' There is always the exception. Phyllis, my neighbour across the corridor, had been a music teacher at some very tough school, and I'll bet she went through hell. She was a burnt-out case all right though not literally. A tiny shrivelled figure, she fizzed and hopped like a firework. She appeared to live just in her nightie and big pink fluffy slippers, and whenever she heard me coming or going she was through her door in a trice, rapping on a pair of castanets.

'Work, Phyllis,' I replied. I'd had a phone call from Penny, who said she had a manuscript to give me and invited me to an address in South Kensington to pick it up. You can't miss it, Penny had said.

She was right about that. In a street of otherwise spacious Victorian villas draped in wisteria, the building in question stood flush with the pavement, a long low edifice with one window protected by an iron grill and a door with iron studs. I rapped on it with the giant brass knocker and was about to flee when

34

Penny opened up. 'Oh hello,' she said brightly. 'You found us then.'

Inside, the hallway was lit by an iron candelabrum, and we appeared to be alone. I stood there quite dumb as Penny handed me a bulky package and said matter-of-factly that it contained the memoirs of an ancient Egyptian princess or priestess. 'I hope it's the kind of thing you're interested in,' she added. Outside again and back in the real world, a Circle Line train rattled past the end of the road.

Phyllis rapped her fingers on her castanets. 'It's a manuscript, isn't it?'

'Yes, Phyllis, it's called *The Wings of Horus*, and now I must fly.'

*

Removed from its wrapping, *The Wings of Horus* was almost a finished book. It was bound in a stiff cover with a pair of silver wings embossed upon a midnight blue. The very stylised hand-written text was photographically reproduced on a kind of parchment and illustrated with dozens of coloured images taken from papyrus scrolls and tomb paintings. Among all the hieroglyphs there was the jackal-headed deity Anubis presiding over the mummified dead, and a menagerie of sacred baboons, cobras, crocodiles, ibises, falcons and scarab beetles.

Adrian peered at the title page. 'Princess Hapshet -' It sounded like he'd sneezed. He tried again. 'Hatepshut.'

'I think it's Hatshepsut.'

'Huh. Well, what's it all about?'

'I think it's meant to be the autobiography of a reincarnated Egyptian princess.'

'Good God.'

'I know.'

'How did you get hold of it?'

'I met this girl Penny at a party, told her where I worked and the kind of books we published, and she seemed interested. Then she phoned up and asked if I'd like to go and collect this.'

'Who is this Penny?'

'I don't really know.'

'What's she like?'

'A bit la-di-dah.'

Adrian sniffed. 'You and your parties.' He glanced at a few more pages and pushed *The Wings of Horus* towards me. 'All right. Better let Brewster see it.'

Also on Adrian's desk, now that Sylvia Bloom was safely out of the way, was the typescript of *Know Your Aura* with Kenneth's report. I pointed to it. 'Doesn't think much of that, does he.'

Adrian nibbled at a fingernail. 'What do you think he means by woolly-minded?'

I shrugged. 'Vague, muddled, sentimental, naive.'

'Is that what you think?'

'Maybe, the bits I've read.'

'All right!' Adrian reached for his claymore. 'But her books sell. We must keep one foot on the ground.'

'By the way, I've met her before.'

'Who are we talking about now?'

'Sylvia Bloom. In my last job. I never spoke to her, but she was on my floor. People there called her Daphne.'

'Daphne!'

'She used to breeze in and out more or less as she pleased and bash away at a typewriter. Probably writing this.'

Adrian looked quite shocked. 'Are you sure it was her?'

'Certain.'

'She didn't seem to know you the other day.'

'I might have surprised her more than she surprised me. You know, blown her cover.'

*

'Got a car?' Kenneth asked. 'Then come down on Sunday for a spot of lunch and bring that thing with you.' I'm sure Penny would have objected to her precious volume being spoken of in such terms. The point was, I didn't want to trust it to the post.

The last time I arrived in Wallingford was by the push-and-pull branch line train that chugged into the station on the far side of town. This time it was by road and from the opposite direction, over the bridge and straight up the High Street. It was a bit of a shock. The bridge, the river beneath it, the handsome spire of St Peter's church, all seemed so much smaller, almost lilliputian. Other landmarks had gone. A lido stood where the old boathouse used to be, with skiffs and punts lapping gently by the water's edge. Early spring sunshine flashed off the perspex and chrome of the cars parked everywhere, crowds wandered aimlessly licking at lollipops and ice creams. Wallingford had gone to hell.

Somehow I remembered to turn right by the Lamb Hotel. I also left the crowds behind, and perhaps just a whiff of the old magic had returned by the time I drove through those portals crowned by two stone griffins and into the Castle grounds. As a child I used to peer round those portals at the large Victorian house with its gothic wing, and a wide circle of lawn with a cypress tree, like a tall black candle, at its centre. If only granny could see me now, I thought, pulling up sharply by some cucumber frames.

'Suzie!' A large salivating dog with a punched-in nose came bounding towards me over the circle of lawn. 'Heel!'

Kenneth, in baggy tweeds, waved a stick. 'Come on over!'

In the entrance hall there was a yawning white marble fireplace and an umbrella stand made from an elephant's foot. Kenneth's wife Elizabeth, also in tweeds, firmly grasped my hand. 'Ken was telling me you know this part of the world.'

'As a boy. My grandmother lived in Wood Street.'

*

Granny was fiercely independent. She'd have nothing to do with doctors, nor, more evidently, with dentists. With only a few blackened stubs of teeth remaining, and no dentures, she tossed the food around her mouth like a cement mixer.

As for her house, standing in the cataleptic calm of Wood Street, it stood independent of time, and once granny had closed the big front door behind you with a bang you had entered another dimension. Maybe it was the fumes from all the wax and polish that made the senses spin. There was the musical box or polyphon in its beautiful little walnut case with copper discs that cracked and snapped as they turned, seeking some other stranger counterpoint in the static air. There was the very old, frayed and yellowed copy of *Struwwelpeter*, with its host of bizarre characters in Victorian garb and strong prime colours, who flew off the page and chased me round the room. There was the mangle, a monstrous contraption of giant wheels and cogs and a handle, that granny wrestled with on wash days as though she were torturing someone on the rack. With hands as red as boiled lobsters she squeezed out the soapy water unless it was blood.

On wet afternoons we used to sit and look out at the old plum tree in the garden till it was so dark we couldn't see each other's face. Then she'd light the gas lamps that burned with a low soft roar, casting a yellow light and deep black shadows around the room. Finally up the stairs by candlelight, to lie wide-eyed between cold sheets in the ringing silence of the night.

*

'Now look here.' Kenneth helped himself to roast potatoes and spoke of Sylvia Bloom. 'She's written herself out. In any case it's the same old woolly-minded nonsense.'

The drive down, the shock of my arrival and that extra-large schooner of sherry before lunch must have left me a bit light-headed. I blurted, 'She said you were a black magician.'

Elizabeth looked up, faintly alarmed. Kenneth dropped his knife and fork with a clatter. 'Yah, yah, yah, yah, yah!' His jaw worked up and down like a ventriloquist's dummy. He wiped the dribble from his mouth with his napkin. 'Look here, I'll show you a few things after lunch.'

A little glass dome in the library roof, like a blister of dreams, cast a halo of light upon the flagstones, and through the latticed windows I spied, across the lawn and beyond the cucumber frames, the battered remains of the small watchtower that I remembered from my many walks along the path through the grounds. Strange to observe the same little scene from the other side of the wall. And was that my childhood ghost somewhere down there?

'Take a look at this.' From a cupboard Kenneth produced a long iron poker with a handle fashioned into a goblin. He needed to grip it with both hands. 'Magic wand,' he said. Not one for conjuring rabbits out of a hat.

He blew the dust off a weighty tome, its thick covers held by a clasp. Leathery pages were filled with weird diagrams and seals. 'Talismans,' Kenneth announced. One of them was all brown and blotched with some lines scratched into it. 'Dried menstrual fluid,' he informed me. He snatched his pipe from his mouth. 'Don't touch it. Never touch a charged talisman!'

I drew my hand back as if it had been stung.

Kenneth struck a match. 'Ever heard of Aleister Crowley?'

The name rang a bell. 'Wasn't he a real black magician?'

Kenneth chuckled quietly. 'Load of nonsense really. The papers called him the wickedest man in the world. Sold a few more copies.'

'So he wasn't a black magician.'

'Played around a bit in that line of country.'

'Did this stuff belong to him?'

'Yes. I knew him when he was stony broke and subbed him a bit. Got hold of it when he died.'

'You seemed to take that talisman quite seriously just now.'

'Can't be too careful.' Kenneth blew through the stem of his pipe and turned to a bulky and most unruly looking manuscript on his desk by a window. 'Now look here. Take this back with you. *The Evil Eye*. Crowley was writing a history of witchcraft. Old friend of mine at Oxford edited and completed it. First class scholarship. Best book on the subject I've come across.'

I'd clean forgotten *The Wings of Horus*. 'Hang on.' I raced back to the car to collect the precious item.

'Chuck it down there.' Kenneth casually scattered ash upon those sacred wings. 'Back home now?'

'I thought I'd just take a quick look in the cemetery. Pay my respects to the family grave.'

*

40

In the luminous light of late afternoon the rooks forever circled above the trees like winged black priests. Passed on, passed on, they intoned. The ground was coated with pine cones and needles, and some of the graves were crowned with little glass domes covering bunches of waxed flowers, long since bleached and turning to dust, like the bones of those beneath. A tall and solitary monkey puzzle tree stood by the one I'd come to see.

Sunday mornings I used to go there with granny to help tend granddad's grave. Strange the way she cared for his grave but never spoke of him, nor kept any memory of him in the house. He'd fought in the First World War, and those few mementoes of him as a soldier were dumped in the old wash house next to the outside toilet.

A ghostly snatch of the Last Post seemed to hover over the picture of him as a sergeant major in the Territorial Army, shiny boots, puttees, tunic and cap, waxed moustache, fingering a drill stick tucked under one arm. His medals were stashed away in an old tin, so glamorous to my young eyes, the large bronze medallions attached to gaudy strips of ribbon. More to the point were two trophies from the Western Front, a German bayonet, more like a knife to gouge out your guts, and a French one, long and slender, to skewer you with.

So what had he been through, as a territorial soldier and one of the first to arrive at the Front? Anywhere out there would have been no picnic, the endless fatigues and still all the spit and polish. But it's the trenches that immediately sprung to mind, the mud, rain, snow and cold, the days and weeks of mind-numbing routine and boredom punctuated by the moments of panic and gut-wrenching fear, and all the time the lousy food, tea brewed with water from a petrol can, barbed wire, lice, fleas, the thousands of rats and millions of flies, trench foot, toothache, diarrhea or constipation, everywhere the smell of death and defecation, and perhaps worst of all, the incessant din of the guns, to drive you screaming mad or reduce you to a shuddering wreck. Shell shock. You prayed for a 'Blighty one', a wound bad enough to get you sent back home. You could imagine, but you could never know.

He'd come through it, though his health was broken. There was another picture of him, just before he died, cradling me in his arms. That's how close I was to him, and so infinitely far away.

Now granny's name was added to his on the marble headstone. Henrietta. She'd had to die before I discovered that. And the monkey puzzle tree was their arboreal guardian, his spiky branches disposed like Medusa's snaky locks, his thick horny trunk planted in a circle of bare black earth, like the foot of a dinosaur. They came from the slopes of the Andes, those strange and exotic trees, from the misty slopes of Conan Doyle's *Lost World*. I couldn't speak for monkeys, but birds kept clear of them. They were a roost for fugitive pterodons.

*

Adrian stifled a yawn. It got hot under the roof some days, and him always in the same dark suit, stiff white collar and tie.

'It's all or nothing with Brewster,' he said wearily. 'And look at the state of it.'

Relieved of its wrapping and its corset of string, the manuscript of *The Evil Eye* had collapsed over Adrian's desk. It had been typed on several different machines, sections of the text were deleted and new ones pasted in, and Kenneth's near indecipherable scrawl much in evidence. And this time he'd accompanied it with a lengthy typewritten report.

42

Adrian began reading it. He suddenly shot forward in his chair. 'Aleister Crowley!'

'That's right. He's mentioned in one or two of our other books.'

'Is he! I must catch up with our backlist.'

'They called him the wickedest man in the world.'

'Crowley?'

'Yes.'

'Who?'

'The press.'

Adrian grabbed his claymore. 'Remember what Sylvia Bloom said?'

'About Crowley?'

'No, Brewster.'

I was glad I hadn't mentioned Kenneth's iron poker or the book of talismans. 'Well, she's a bit potty.'

'Huh.' Adrian tried shuffling the contents of *The Evil Eye* together. 'Anyway,' he sighed, 'we can't do anything with it in this state. Can you try and sort it out?'

I nodded. 'Perhaps Cindy had better retype it.'

'You don't think it's too much for her?'

'The contents or the typing?'

'Both!'

'I'll keep an eye on her.'

I turned to the typescript of *Know Your Aura*, still resting on Adrian's desk. 'Talking of Sylvia Bloom, like me to cast that off?'

Adrian toyed with his claymore. 'Not just yet.'

'Thinking of chucking it out?'

'What!' For a moment he looked quite scared. 'Look, I'll admit the writing's a bit slapdash. Could do with some brushing up here and there. Perhaps we can talk about that.'

'Glad to.' I carried the *The Evil Eye* next door, dropping pages on the way.

Cindy meantime had taken a phone call. She clapped a hand over the instrument and in some excitement mouthed the words, 'Sylvia Bloom'. We couldn't get away from her.

'No big deal,' I said in a low voice. 'Just put her through to Adrian.'

A tricky little telephonic operation, but Cindy managed it. She started to unwrap a chocolate bar. 'Watcher got there?'

'It's a manuscript called *The Evil Eye*, *A History of Witchcraft*, and you may have to do some work on it.'

'Any pictures?'

'Lots.'

She was over like a shot. 'Wot's goin' on here, then?'

'I think it's a medieval woodcut of witches at a Sabbath, kissing the Devil's backside.'

'Blimey! When he said you can kiss my arse, he meant it!'

'Yes, and mind where you're dribbling.'

The door opened and Adrian poked his head round it. 'If that woman rings again, I'm OUT.'

*

Several light years separated that bizarre place in South Kensington from my pad, mattress on the floor with a few crumpled bed clothes, one chair, a couple of mugs, a couple of glasses, kettle, old gas cooker in the adjoining kitchen area. And I reckoned I knew which one Penny felt more at home in.

She sat in the chair, a glass of wine in her hand, *The Wings of Horus* on her lap, and looked down at me, reclining on the mattress at her feet.

'I'm sorry,' I said. Kenneth had returned to his town house and brought *The Wings of Horus* back with him.

Penny took another sip of wine. 'So what did he actually say, your literary adviser?'

'I'm afraid that's confidential.'

Penny fluttered her eyelashes and sweetly inclined her head. 'You can tell me.'

'He said she's as nutty as a fruitcake.'

'Oh!'

'There you are, I knew you wouldn't like it. And for God's sake keep it to yourself.'

'My lips are sealed.'

'By the way, who is she? Princess what's-her-name?'

'I'm afraid I can't tell you that.'

'Come on, tit for tat.'

'No really.'

'All right, what's that strange house you invited me to? Is that where she lives?'

'Yes, well some of the time.'

'Was she there when I called?'

'No, she also has a place in the country.'

Everybody seemed to have a place in the country but me. 'So what's your connection?'

Penny shifted in the chair. 'I do a few things for The Children of Osiris. Sort of secretarial.'

'The what?'

'The Children of Osiris. I knew you'd laugh.'

'I'm not laughing. So who are these people?'

'Just a small group interested in the religions of ancient Egypt.'

'Are you interested too?'

Penny shrugged. 'So so,' she said and quickly changed the subject. She pointed down at my pillow. 'What's that?'

'Who's that, you mean. That's Blunderbuss.' I picked up the little object beside me. 'All grey and smoky you see, like he was looking into one when it went off.'

'I've still got some of my old pets.'

'He's not really a pet. Well, I suppose he is. A little orphan of the storm. I found him a while ago, on a cold wet day, strapped to the front of a truck, roasted one minute, frozen the next, covered in grease and grime, forgotten by the whole rotten world. The truck was parked, so I ran back here, got my scissors, ran back and cut him down.'

'Like Christ from the Cross.'

'If you like.'

'Perhaps you were feeling a bit low at the time and saw something of yourself in him.' Penny leaned forward and I handed Blunderbuss up to her. She inspected him at arm's length, little legs dangling down in what remained of his red and white striped trousers, little red button eyes meeting her gaze.

'He's rather small for a bear.'

I put a finger to my lips. 'With that colour and that face,' I whispered confidentially, 'I think he's probably a mouse. But if he thinks he's a bear that's okay with me.'

'Absolutely!' Penny whispered back. Through the window an aircraft winked and blinked its way across the twilit sky. She watched it for a moment. 'Are you going to get some curtains?'

'I was thinking of blinds.'

'Yes, blinds would be nice,' she said, sitting Blunderbuss on her knee and making him nod his little grey head.

*

There must be hundreds of churches and chapels like the one that was ten minutes' walk from my place, Victorian piles of gothic stone and flint calling down the same cold and unforgiving sky, as if heaven itself was somewhere to be endured. On its damp and sunless plot this one was rather more than that, unless I'd been thinking a bit too much about Kenneth and his bits and pieces. Watch for a feverish flicker of light behind those grimy windows, listen for the muffled scream of some satanic rite. Then silence, night and rain.

That is till you walked round to the front and stepped through the new plate glass doors. Inside, spotlights shone down upon a polished pinewood floor, neat rows of chairs and raised dais with two large loudspeakers. The venue of our local music club.

All the same, on that particular evening there was something murky, something demonic in the music presently coming from those loudspeakers, the febrile skips and runs on the piano, and the harmonies, weird and unhinged. A few grey heads among the audience, more used to Mendelssohn, began to nod.

They jerked awake with the scattering of applause that greeted the end of the piece. We'd been listening to Scriabin. The cafeteria serving hatch at the back of the hall came up with a rattle of relief and we formed a ragged queue for coffee and biscuits.

Well I'd be damned. I took a step forward and tapped her on the shoulder. 'Evening, Iris.'

She spun round. 'Good Lord! I say, hello!'

'What brings you to this den of iniquity?'

'I've known Ingrid for ages. It's her show.'

'Is that the large lady who gave the vote of thanks and made a few announcements?'

The lady in question waved at us from across the hall. Iris waved back.

I said, 'I'd have thought Scriabin and all that occult stuff was a bit much for this bunch.'

'I know, but the speaker's an old flame of hers from the BBC.'

'A touch of the black widow spider there, I'd say.'

'What?'

'Black widow spider. You know, the female eats her mate after copulation. I mean, Ingrid could eat him for breakfast.'

'Keep your voice down!'

'Incidentally, didn't you once work for the BBC?'

'Yes.'

'Is that where you met her?'

'Yes!'

'Where's Sam, by the way?'

Iris stepped out of the queue. 'Listen, let's go and have a decent drink.'

We settled for the nearest pub. 'He was the laziest sod I ever met,' she said.

'Was?'

'He was supposed to be writing the music for some West End show, but I never heard a note of it. He almost never touched that piano either. Lying in bed most of the time.'

'So what's happened to him?'

'I gave him the old heave-ho.'

'Talking of bed, I thought he was supposed to be good in it.'

'That's beside the point.'

'What about his piano?'

'My piano, if you don't mind. I mean it is now. I'm still paying for it on the old drip-feed.'

'Do you play?'

'That's not the point!'

Outside the pub again a fine drizzle filled the air and tyres hissed on freshly wet tarmac. Overhead, with a rising scream, an aircraft probed the low cloud base with the beam of its landing lights.

'He was going to teach me chord signs. Remember?'

'Who?'

'Sam.'

Iris fiddled with her umbrella. 'Look, can we change the subject.'

*

A telephone came with the flat. It shared the floor with my mattress and so far Penny was the only person who had the number. She called to ask if I'd done anything about some blinds. Yes, and would she like to come round and let me know what she thought of them.

'They're a sort of sea green,' she said approvingly. 'Very restful.'

'Good,' I replied from the mattress, with another bottle of wine to hand. 'Now tell me, what do you know about Scriabin?'

'Who?'

'Thought I'd spring that one on you!'

Alexander Scriabin, I told her, was a Russian composer who lived during the early years of the twentieth century. He was also a great pianist. His early piano pieces weren't very original, sounding quite like Chopin. Then he became interested in the occult and this inspired him to compose some of the most extraordinary and technically advanced music of his time.

'I've never heard of him.'

'Well, you have now. At one time he was mixed up with a group of Satanists who may have practised cannibalism.'

'Heavens!'

'I'm not saying he did, Penny. Scriabin's main interest was in Theosophy. Have you heard of that?'

Penny furrowed her brow and thought hard. 'I think so.'

I'd read up a bit about Theosophy as well. It was founded by another Russian, a spiritualist named Madame Blavatsky, as a kind of occult religion, mixing spiritualism with bits and pieces of all the other religions, and during Scriabin's lifetime it was a big thing. There were branches of the Theosophical Society everywhere. It inspired Scriabin to write such pieces as *The Poem of Fire* and *The Poem of Ecstasy* for orchestra and his *Black Mass Sonata* for the piano.

'Black Mass!' Penny exclaimed.

I nodded. 'But that wasn't all. Scriabin was also fascinated by what he saw as the connection between sounds, music and colour. He called the key of D major golden brown, and another note he described as a glint of steel. He invented a colour keyboard. As you played the notes and harmonies it projected patterns of colours onto a wall or screen.'

'That,' said Penny, 'sounds rather beautiful.'

'Yes, but he lost his marbles in the end. He planned a colossal work for orchestra and choruses called *Mysterium* which he wanted performed in a kind of temple way up in the Himalayan Mountains. The temple was to be built as a giant hemisphere surrounding a lake, so that when you were inside it the reflection of the water would create the illusion of a complete sphere, that is, the cosmos.'

'I say!'

'Scriabin also spoke about bells hanging from the clouds. I mean, he totally flipped. He thought he was a new Messiah. I am God, he said. And do you know what happened to him, Penny? He died from blood poisoning after he cut a pimple on his lip while he was shaving. Just shows you, doesn't it.'

We considered for a few moments what this showed us.

'Talking of colours,' Penny said next, 'I wonder what Scriabin would have made of your blinds, what note he'd have played to them.'

'I wonder.'

'You should write a book about him.'

'It's been done, hasn't it. I mean, where do you think I got all this information from?'

'If it's from encyclopedias, then they're not the same thing. I mean a real book, perhaps not just about Scriabin but about music and the occult. Music and magic. There must be lots to say!'

'I don't know how to write a book.'

'You won't know till you try.'

*

As a matter of fact I had tried, as a child and growing up, poetry, stories, drawing too, or sketching as I called it. My mum and dad let me get on with it, neither praising nor criticising my efforts. He'll grow out of it. But I hadn't, not entirely. Something was always there, something bugging me, scratching at my mind, the way I saw things, buildings, landscapes, the sky, often with pieces of music attached. Something waiting to break out, to express itself.

Now suddenly here was Penny, throwing down the gauntlet. Let's see what I was made of. After so long a period of hibernation, how to start and where to start. By putting pen or pencil to paper, of course. The moment of truth and one of the toughest things in the world to do. To start.

Lying on my mattress, head propped up by a pillow and a large book from the office to rest a sheet of paper on, pencil poised as though deciding whether or not to jump, I wrote bravely at the top of it, Music and Magic. Go on. Write anything. Music, I scribbled, is a kind of magic. You can't see it or touch it. It's just in the air, like the wind. Don't stop. Keep going. Music's also hard-wired in our blood. A mother croons to her baby. The baby goes to sleep. Sing it a song and it'll laugh or want to dance. Singing, clapping, shouting, dancing to summon courage to hunt wild beasts or call on the gods and spirits to bring sunshine or rain. Caveman stuff, but it's the spirit of music.

I stopped for a moment, quite dizzy in the head. How to go on. I jotted down a few notes. Musical instruments. The oldest human artefact yet found, a bone flute reckoned to be 40,000 years old. Ancient tribal drums and flutes made from skin and bone. Play them and you summon up the spirit of the dead animal, human or otherwise. No wonder they were regarded with such awe, the property of the witchdoctor or shaman. Your music and magic taking shape.

The ancient Greeks and their sacred muses, inspiring song and dance. That must be where our word 'music' comes from. Orpheus taming the wild beasts with song, the great god Apollo with his lyre, the story of Pan and Syrinx and the famous pipes. And in the Bible, what about those ram's horns or whatever bringing down the walls of Jericho. Music and religion, much the same thing as magic.

A pause, to get my breath back and watch an aircraft glide across the sky. Then let's look at it another way. Think about all those pieces of music, all those operas, ballets, symphonies, and the rest, inspired by magic and the occult, curses and spells, ghosts, demons, and all that jazz. *The Magic Flute, The Flying Dutchman, Lohengrin, Der Freischütz, Swan Lake, The Firebird, Night on the Bare Mountain, The Sorcerer's Apprentice.* Faust and his pact with the Devil and what composers like Liszt made of him (Mephisto Waltzes). Scriabin! A whole bloody chapter on him.

My God, once you got started, how it all tumbled out. I was also absolutely knackered. And, bloody hell, was that the time!

*

'Morning, Phyllis.' There she was, in nightie and fluffy slippers, out in the corridor with a piece of music on her radio. A Haydn quartet, it sounded like, with castanets.

I asked her, 'Have you heard of something called The Music or the Harmony of the Spheres?'

She stopped in mid clack. I'll bet nobody had asked her a serious question, about music or anything else, in years. For a moment she looked suspicious, as though it might have been some sort of a trap. Then she was off, about Ptolemy and the ancient notion of the stars and planets, then about Pythagoras and the basis of sound. It was a real lecture, of the kind she'd never been able to give. I stood and listened, quite spellbound.

'Phyllis, you amaze me.'

I think she'd amazed herself. Running down the stairs because I was late, she was right behind me. 'Anyway, what's all this about?'

'Oh, just a bit of research.'

At the front door she began again on the castanets, the sound of them following me down the street like the chattering of teeth in a graveyard. Saint-Saëns' *Danse Macabre*. Another one for the pot.

*

Kenneth took off his hat, leaving a rim round his thick and unruly head of hair. The manuscript of *Know Your Aura* still languished on Adrian's desk after his last encounter with Sylvia Bloom on the phone.

'Now look here.' Kenneth struck a match. 'It doesn't really matter how badly it's written. It'll sell to the woolly minded with her name on it.'

Adrian bridled. 'I must say that's a rather cynical attitude to take.'

Kenneth held his matchbox over the bowl of his pipe, sucked and chuckled. 'How's *The Evil Eye* coming along?'

'I'm having it re-typed for a start. Try and get some sort of order into it.'

'Good idea.'

Adrian reached for his claymore. 'Aleister Crowley was a pretty notorious character, wasn't he?'

'He had a lot of women, got kicked out of Sicily. But he was a fine scholar at Cambridge. Studied all the major religions. Travelled the world. Climbed several mountains. Knew a lot of people. Somerset Maughan.'

'Really?'

'Ian Fleming.'

'The James Bond author?'

'Yes. He may have worked for British Intelligence himself. Mind you, by the time I met him he was in a pretty poor way. Stony broke and on heroine.'

'You knew him!'

'Yes.'

Adrian took a few moments to digest this. He obviously still didn't know about the poker and the book of talismans. 'Anyway,' he said, getting back to the matter in hand, 'it's going to cost a bomb to produce. What with the text and all those illustrations.'

Kenneth blew through the stem of his pipe. 'Won't matter how much it costs. Just jack up the price. A book like that will sell on its merits and for years. A classic of its kind.'

Adrian ran a hand through his hair and took a deep breath. 'All right, I might as well tell both of you now. We've had next year's budget slashed by nearly a half.'

Kenneth continued serenely, 'Now look here, I've been in touch with this Japanese Zen master. Could be a decent little book in him. Won't cost much and there's a growing market in that field. Sell like hot cakes.' He put his hat back on.

'What,' I dared to ask, 'about a book on music and magic?'

'Music.' Kenneth snapped shut his case. 'Not my line of country.'

*

Next door, Cindy had found an old pack of Tarot cards and had pushed aside the massive typescript of *The Evil Eye* to lay them out on her desk. The Philosopher, the Fool, Death, the Hermit, suns and moons and stars, oceans and mountains and thunderbolts, tall towers tumbling down. Those cards had the same strong prime colours and lines as the pictures in *Struwwelpeter*, simple but compelling, tapping into the collective unconscious. They'd make a great ballet, the Tarot or *Struwwelpeter*. Talking of ballets, hadn't someone written music for a ballet called *Horoscope*? And now we'd moved onto astrology, there was also *The Planets Suite* by Gustav Holst. Music and Astrology. That could almost be a book in itself, what with The Harmony of the Spheres (thank you Phyllis) and everything.

'Going to tell my fortune, Cindy?' She turned up another card. 'The Hanged Man,' I said. 'That looks ominous.'

'Not 'alf!' she agreed.

*

'Such a shame poor Iris has the flu.' Ingrid of the music club had invited Iris and myself to one of her musical soirees. She lived in a large Edwardian house of apoplectic red brick that had been divided into flats. An external iron staircase and balcony led to hers. She waved me inside. 'Still, I'm so glad you could make it.'

She led me by the hand into her living room, her hair now dressed in one long plait that hung over her shoulder. 'I think you know most of us.' Some of them I recognised from the music club, and we shuffled around till I fell into an armchair beneath a collection of glass paper-weights and an oriental Laughing Buddha.

One face was new to me. It belonged to someone who'd taken her shoes off and occupied part of a couch, legs and feet tucked under her shapely little peach of a bum in the manner of Hans Andersen's Little Mermaid. She wasn't all that young or especially pretty, but there was something etched into her face, some part of her that made me believe she'd entertained the same sort of secret and nameless fantasies as a child, and she knew that I knew. We held each other's gaze for one long second, till Ingrid, with a guitar slung round her neck, pulled up a large white pouffe and plopped herself down between us. She sang 'The Foggy Foggy Dew' tolerably well, while we handed round the coconut creams.

At the end of it Ingrid unslung the guitar and clapped her hands. 'Now who's for musical scrabble!' The words all had to be the names of composers, conductors and other artists, compositions, musical terms and expressions, that sort of thing.

I'd once played a game of scrabble that I'd rather forget, with someone I couldn't forget. Let's just say that I'd taken against it in any shape or form. A game, I rationalised, for people who could play with words but couldn't use them. Most unfair.

I struggled out of my chair. 'You'll have to excuse me but I think I'd better have an early night. Office meeting first thing in the morning.'

At her front door Ingrid said in a low voice, 'You must come round again soon for a bite to eat. Tell me more about yourself.'

And how about The Little Mermaid. Imagine her face if I'd joined in the scrabble and put down the name of that Polish composer. Szymanowski, was it? The face that said to me, it takes one to know one. Whatever that might mean to the both of us.

*

Penny, back once more on my chair, wanted to know how my book was getting on, so I thought I might as well show off. 'What do you know about Pythagoras?' I asked.

Penny furrowed her brow. 'Didn't he invent a theorem or something?'

'Yes, about squares on the hypotenuse of right-angled triangles, I think, but he did a lot more than that, Penny.'

I told her that like just about everyone else in the ancient world, the Babylonians and Chaldeans - the three wise men in the Bible were probably Chaldean astrologers - the Egyptians, the Greeks and Romans, and all the rest of them, Pythagoras believed in something called The Music or The Harmony of the Spheres. This was a kind of celestial harmony, or divine order, that governed everything in the universe, the sun, moon, planets and stars in their courses, everything here on earth as well as up above.

What Pythagoras did was to experiment with actual sounds, like the different pitches of a set of bells, or a scale of notes produced by changing the length of a vibrating string, and then work out the mathematical proportions between the notes, how high or low in pitch one note was to another. That way he was one of the first people we know of to investigate the scientific properties of sound, speeds of vibration related to the pitch of notes, that sort of thing. What his experiments were all in aid of was to try and discover the mathematics of the Harmony of the Spheres and the order of the universe. 'At least, I think that's what he was after. My mind's spinning trying to make sense of it all.'

'Like one of those spheres.'

'Like one of those spheres.' I topped up our glasses. 'Anyway, it's terrific stuff, isn't it? A wonderful harmony up there among the stars and planets. But it doesn't end with people like Pythagoras. This notion of a perfect harmony or order governing everything haunted the greatest artists and thinkers for centuries to come.' I started to list them on my fingers. 'Galileo, Leonardo da Vinci, Michelangelo, Copernicus, Johann Kepler, Isaac Newton, Descartes, just to name a few, they all tuned into this idea of a Harmony of the Spheres.'

Penny added cautiously, 'It's not quite musical magic though, is it? Not like Scriabin and Black Mass sonatas.'

'It's all connected, Penny.' I pointed to the pages of notes I'd made, next to me on the floor. 'You know, astrology and all that jazz.'

She heaved a dramatic sigh. 'I'm amazed!'

'I know, but whatever I said about my mind spinning, that's still the easy part. How to tie it all together, turn it into a proper theme or argument for a book, that's the bottom line. That's the crunch.'

'You can't hurry these things.'

'You can say that again. Everybody's in such a bloody rush all the time these days. Think of people like Ptolemy and Pythagoras and Galileo gazing up at the night sky for hours, for weeks and months and years, patiently observing and plotting the tiniest differences in the movements of the planets.'

'What about the nights when it was cloudy?'

'They got pissed.'

Penny laughed, a true belly laugh, spontaneous, unguarded. She wasn't such a Little Miss Muffet after all. She knew the world was mad. The wine had also brought a flush to her face and seemed to have smoothed away some of those little wrinkles. Supposing I suddenly reached up and pulled her off the chair and down onto the mattress on top of me? Was she half hoping that I would? There we were, talking mathematics and astronomy and mysticism and aesthetics and God knows what else, and still hung up by our sad little bourgeois inhibitions.

'Wine.' I raised my glass to her. 'Smoothing away the wrinkles of the mind.'

'Who said that?'

'I just did.'

*

Adrian could have done with a good stiff whisky. Tense and pale at the best of times, he now looked a bit like a man about to be hanged, though not like the one on Cindy's tarot card who was dangling upside down by one leg. He hesitated before he broke the news.

'I should have seen it coming when they slashed our budget,' he said in a lifeless voice. It was Omega. The end.

'They gave me another year to show a profit,' he said in a listless monotone, 'but they couldn't even wait that long. Nobody's given any time to do anything these days. It's instant results or you're out. It's not even that. You're just a figure in somebody's statement of accounts. It's all accountants now.'

Stirring in his chair, Adrian tossed his claymore down in a symbolic act of surrender. 'There's no soul in publishing any more. Just balance sheets and takeovers. We might as well be selling cornflakes!'

In the heavy silence, sounds intruded from the outside world, a dog barking in the street, a fit of the giggles from somewhere down below.

I asked, 'Told anyone else yet?'

Adrian shook his head.

'Kenneth? Sylvia Bloom?'

'God, not her'.

'Like me to tell Cindy?'

'Yes,' he said with a deep sigh. 'She likes you. Break it to her gently.'

Next door Cindy was still busily retyping *The Evil Eye* and loving every minute of it.

'Here, that old Aleister Crowley, he must 'ave got up to a few tricks.'

'I'll bet he did.'

'And listen, I know what them Grimoires mean now. Books on magic, how to cast spells, summon up demons. All that creepy stuff.'

'I know.'

'And pentagrams. You can cast magical spells with them, an' all.'

'Right. Anyway Cindy you can stop now.'

'Got a letter to dash off?'

I shook my head. 'We're packing in.'

'You mean we're not going to publish it?'

'No, I mean we're going out of business. Adrian's just told me. We're just a tiny cog in some great big corporation and they've decided we're not important enough.'

Cindy was also silent for a moment. Then she said, as though the news hadn't quite sunken in, 'But when I first came here Adrian told me we was on the up and up. Really going places.'

'I know. But that's how quickly things can change. In any case, you don't have to worry. Everyone's crying out for temps these days.'

Cindy's face suddenly blazed. 'So I'm just a temp am I!' Her eyes swam with tears and mascara ran down her chubby cheeks. 'I could have been earning a bloody sight more money somewhere else but I kept asking the agency to let me stay 'ere. I liked you lot!'

She jumped up, knocking over her chair, rushed from the room and into the toilet, slamming the door behind her. There was the loud rasp of the bolt, a sound of sobbing, and the noisy blowing of a nose.

Adrian looked in. 'What's going on?'

'Cindy took it badly. You can never tell with people, can you?'

'Oh yes you can.' Adrian suddenly snapped right back into life. 'She's cancer. All the high spirits are just a shell. Crack that open and she's hopelessly vulnerable underneath.'

'What about you?'

'Taurus.' Adrian stiffened. 'Like the Queen.'

I must have read it somewhere. 'And Adolf Hitler.'

'What!'

Poor Cindy seemed to have cleared the air a bit.

*

Taurus types, I read, were conservative by nature, they liked things as they were, they were also home loving, loyal but sometimes stubborn, and if really provoked they could suddenly lose their rag like a bull. So that was Adrian, Hitler and the Queen.

Of course, Taurus was only their sun sign within the order of the zodiac. I'd been doing some reading up on astrology, all grist to the mill with Music and Magic, and learnt there was a lot more to it than that. Your date, time and place of birth, and the corresponding position of the sun, moon and all the other planets (their conjunctions and oppositions, I think they were called) all played a big part in shaping the kind of person you were. So that you could end up a very complicated, mixed-up kid indeed.

And how about being born on a 'cusp', which is what Adrian said had happened to me. That is, being born right between two sun signs. Could that explain the pull and tug of my character, often wanting to do one thing and doing the other? Or when things went wrong suddenly and deliberately making them worse. Or when someone or something pushed me over some sort of limit and I was suddenly locked into a state of mind where I could hardly speak, hardly do anything, while a huge weight inside just dragged me down. Was that all to do with my cusp? Or was it all just more of what Iris called her mumbo jumbo?

Whether there was any truth in it or not, astrology was a vast and fascinating subject, going back in history hundreds or thousands of years. The people of China and India, the Aztecs and Mayans of Mexico, the Incas of Peru, all wondered at the heavens and read into the constellations of the stars, the movements of the planets, the moon and the sun, a guide for life down here on Earth. As above, so below.

And look at all that colourful imagery and language, the zodiac and those sun signs, the crab, the scorpion, the bull, and the rest of them, fancifully related to the starry constellations and bound up with so much myth and legend. Look at those horoscopes, the circles with all their arcane signs and numbers and the criss-crossing patterns of lines within them, creating a geometry the like of which left Euclid and Pythagoras miles behind.

From staring out of the window I gazed back at the sheet of paper in front of me. Pythagoras and the Harmony of the Spheres, I jotted down. Gustav Holst and *The Planets Suite*. Well, make something out of that.

*

What, I wondered, was Ingrid's sun sign? A black widow spider, remembering what I'd said at that Music Club evening, eating her mate after they'd had it off.

Having it off? Ingrid wobbled over me with breasts like those of her Laughing Buddha and nipples brown and flat as cow pats. There was a good deal of pungent bodily fluid that didn't emanate from me. I was dry as a bone.

'I'm sorry,' I gasped, pinned down by those mighty thighs. I didn't touch the sides.

Ingrid came slowly off the boil and rolled over to one side, reaching for her tissues. Still in my vest, I grabbed my other clothes and shoes and fled to the bathroom. A celluloid doll draped over the spare toilet roll looked infinitely more desirable after what I'd just experienced.

Stuffing my shirt into my trousers, I paused at the bedroom door and said, 'I think I'd better be going.'

'That's right, get back to your teddy bears!' Ingrid whipped round with tears in her eyes and hurled a hairbrush at me. If it had been one of those Victorian paperweights, and if her aim had been better, it could have been curtains for me.

I clattered down the balcony stairs, sped across the road and into my car, lowering the window and sucking in the raw night air to feed a racing heart.

Why had I accepted her invitation for supper? Why not? For one mad split second I might even have fancied her. It must have been the booze. Was Ingrid a nymphomaniac, or just desperately lonely? Could be both. Poor woman. After what had happened I could still feel sorry for her. On the other hand, what was that snide remark about teddy bears? She'd better not start on Blunderbuss, that's all.

*

I lay back on the mattress with him by the pillow, gazed at my picture and gradually felt better. I'd bought it from the junk shop round the corner, rescued it from the dank and musty clutter of old chairs and sofas with the stuffing knocked out of them, discarded hats and clothes and shoes, jig saw puzzles, old board games, a ping pong bat, an ancient transistor radio, a large selection of mildewed paperbacks. The old guy didn't know what to ask for it. Five pounds? Done!

How had such a picture ended up there in the first place? It was a fairly small watercolour. The hulk of a large sailing ship with its masts broken off was stranded on a beach. The angry sea that cast it there had now retreated to an innocent line of blue, where two other small white sails billowed from afar. Gulls wheeled among misty banks of cloud, with a chilly hint of early morning sun. People were gathered round the wreck and a top-hatted gentleman on horseback looked on. Others were going about their business, a fisherman with his nets, a man with horse and cart, gathering seaweed. And in the foreground was a rock pool with two stumps of wood, like rotting teeth in a scurvy gum.

*

'Teeth in a scurvy gum,' Penny mused. 'You have a very vivid way of putting things.'

'But do you like it? The picture, I mean?'

'Oh yes! It just looks a bit lonely all on its own on the wall.'

'It's got to be an original, not a copy of anything. It looks like the frame's original as well.'

'Where did you get it?'

'From an old junk shop round the corner. For a fiver.'

'Gosh!'

'I know. Maybe it's painted from life.'

Penny inspected it closely. 'Yes. Early nineteenth century, I'd say.'

'Regency then. Could be Brighton, or Brightelmstone as I think it was called when it was still a fishing village. My home town, you know.'

'Is it?'

'Well, Hove actually, but they're almost the same place, and Brighton has more of a ring to it, don't you think?'

'Definitely!'

'Have you been there?'

'Yes. I once went for a ride on Volk's Electric Railway.'

'There's that, and the Palace Pier, the Royal Pavilion, the Lanes, Marine Parade, Black Rock. You only really appreciate a place when you've left it. I was a cub reporter on the local paper. *The Evening Argus.*'

'How thrilling!'

'You think so, Penny?' I told her about the AGMs I had to cover, Annual General Meetings, of all the local societies and clubs, usually held in some cold gloomy room over a pub. With any luck they started more or less on time but soon got bogged down with the Statement of Accounts or Any Other Business. There was always some busybody too fond of their own voice who went on and on and I couldn't leave till it was all over, just in case someone had a heart attack or the place caught fire, which would have made a story. Then back to the offices to scrape out a couple of pointless sentences about what a successful year they'd had and nearly miss the last bus home.

Schools sports days, standing on the edge of some muddy wind-swept field while the events fell further and further behind schedule, then back again to knock out all those results, the number of records broken, then first, second, third, long jump, high jump, hop, skip and a bloody jump, distances and times, and woe betide me if I got some brat's name wrong, even the initials, because their parents would be on the phone the next day, kicking up a fuss.

'You've quite shattered my illusions,' Penny said.

I added a bit about the offices, brick walls painted a kind of smudgy brown and green like an old-fashioned prison, the fly-blown light bulbs, the stench of stale tobacco and hot metal from the typesetting machines and the dust that danced about when they ran the machines downstairs.

First night on a Monday at the old Grand Theatre was different. They sent me because it didn't matter. Anyway, there I sat, in the front row of the stalls, close enough to see the worn-out corduroys beneath the bass player's tuxedo and watch him munch on a sandwich as he scraped away at 'There's No Business Like Show Business', the patches on the chorus girls' tights and their ageing flesh begin to wobble, the sweat running down the greasepaint on the comic's face as he struggled to get a laugh in that cold, half empty auditorium. Then I'd go back to that crummy office and say what fun it all was.

'Oh dear.'

For a few moments we watched the silent procession of aircraft drifting across the sky towards Heathrow.

'They had titles like 'Strip Strip Hooray' and 'Don't Point It's Nude''.

'What did?' Penny asked.

'The shows at the Grand Theatre.'

'Did they really have nudes?'

'One or two sometimes, standing at the back of the stage, catching cold. Mustn't move, you see, not in those days.'

'Even if they sneezed?'

'Nope.'

*

What I should have written about was what I really saw up there on the stage of the Grand Theatre, the death throes of the old music hall and all those shattered hopes and dreams. That's what true writing was about, wasn't it? Real life, the sight, sound, smell, taste and touch of it, experiencing it, then letting it settle in the mind, letting it incubate, before trying to put it into words. A very private and solitary business too. At any rate, not wrestling with the Harmony of the Spheres and Pythagoras and the rest of that nebulous stuff.

'You look tired this morning.' Phyllis was waiting as usual with the castanets. She must have fingers and nails of steel.

'Doing a bit of work last night.'

'I thought you'd lost your job.'

'Nothing to do with that.'

'What then?'

'Just making a few notes.'

'It's a book, isn't it?'

'Maybe, maybe not.'

'It's about the Harmony of the Spheres, isn't it?'

'As a matter of fact Phyllis I don't know what the hell it's about.'

'I tried writing a book once, a novel. Drove me bonkers!'

Phyllis could say that again, and not just because it was her. I was beginning to think that writing a book could drive anybody round the bend.

She was down the stairs behind me, clackety clack. 'You're looking smart anyhow. I like the tie. Going somewhere special?'

'Got an interview.'

'For a new job?'

'What else.'

*

I don't think it was the cusp this time, so let's say it was the tie, smart but not flash. You could say that with even more certainty of Dr Gutt, founder and managing director of The Medical Library Press. His clothes had the look of Savile Row, while his broad pate, still graced with a few strands of hair, shone with some rare pomade.

His words, though not his voice, were a faint echo of Adrian's first words to me. His firm, he said, had once led the field in medical books. But he was not so young anymore and he had allowed things to slip. That's where I would come in. I didn't need to know anything about medicine. What he needed was someone with publishing experience and the kind of drive and initiative needed to clear up the present log jam of work. His accent thickened as he warmed to his theme. 'You will haff to crack zer whip!' he declared. And he had a special title for me as well. Project Controller.

*

I couldn't blame Jock for being cagey. I tried a bit of chat. 'You can't see the Tower from down here then.' It didn't work, nor deserved to. Through the iron bars across Jock's window and the pavement railings all you could see were the feet and legs of passers- by.

Production Department stretched back in deepest gloom to a far window staring at a brick wall. A few empty desks and chairs were scattered about, as though there had been a sudden exit. Jock's own desk, by contrast, and the floor space around it, was piled high with sagging manuscripts and batches of proofs, settled like compacted snow. Try pulling anything from that lot and you'd start an avalanche.

'You're kept pretty busy, then.'

Jock, curly pipe stuck in his mouth, carried on working. 'Aye.'

I checked my publishing schedule. 'I see that galley proofs for *Disorders of the Thyroid* are due next week.'

'Aye.'

'Give us a word as soon as they arrive.'

'Aye.'

'Right, see you later.'

I climbed back up the stone steps from the basement to the hallway, with its gilded mirror, black and white tiled floor, dark red carpet and fanlight over the big front door. Onwards and upwards, the carpet soon ran out, the stairs changed from marble to wood, becoming narrower and creakier and more precipitous as they neared the top. A final door had a streak of light beneath it, where once some lowly housemaid might have shivered in her bed. An ascent in social history.

Editorial, it now said on that attic door. I went over to the small square window. 'Can you see the Tower from up here?'

'Round the corner, mate,' Ted replied.

'What's all the smoke over there?'

'University College Hospital.'

'I thought this was a smokeless zone.'

'Amputations day.' Ted crushed out his cigarette.

'You mean they've got an incinerator for all those limbs and things?'

'What would you do with 'em?' He was working on a manuscript containing what looked like some pretty tough mathematics.

I had another look at my schedule. 'Is that, er, *Medical Endoscopy*?'

'Got it in one, mate.'

'Shall we say ready for setting next Thursday?'

'We can say that.'

'That's the twenty first.' The girl on Ted's calendar, pinned to the door, had gigantic knockers. 'Too big for me,' I added.

'And me, mate.'

Metal bookshelves, assembled with nuts and bolts, were kept upright by a wooden wedge at one end. The floor sloped towards the window.

'By the way, who sits over there?' I pointed to another chair, a high one, behind a drawing board.

'Percy, when he's around. Does line drawings when we need 'em, but its mostly colour pictures we want, better for showin' up the blood.'

'Right. So what is Medical Endoscopy? I've heard of fibre optics.'

'Not the same thing, mate.'

'What's the difference?'

'Endoscopy is stickin' a light up yer arse.' Ted stuck a fresh cigarette in his mouth and grinned, his teeth stained the colour of old piano keys. 'Among other apertures.'

*

You had to step across the Square to see the Tower, a giant shiny propelling pen, and near the top of it a thin shaft of sunlight struck an answering gleam. Scriabin's glint of steel.

He wasn't alone with his thoughts and feelings about sounds and colours. One of my first toys was a musical top. You set it spinning and it hummed like the Harmony of the

71

Spheres, creating for me a whole rainbow of sounds. Later on, years before Scriabin came on the scene, I associated different chords and keys with different colours or shades. D minor was a coal-fire red, F major a harvest yellow, G major grass green, C minor dark brown, E flat major gold, B flat major sky blue. Whole symphonies and other compositions in this or that key acquired such colours and textures in my mind. I told my mum about it one day. 'How peculiar!' she said.

Something else I did was to put my ear to those old wooden telegraph poles and hear another kind of ethereal humming sound. I fancied it was the sound of the electric power running through the cables. Much more likely, it was the sound as they vibrated in the wind being transmitted down the wooden pole.

That was the principle of the aeolian harp. Named after Aeolus, the ancient Greek Keeper of the Winds, you didn't pluck the strings of such a harp. You placed it somewhere to catch the wind then listened to the strings vibrate and perhaps fancifully capture the voice of Aeolus himself. In truth the majority of such instruments didn't look like harps but more like a kind of zither, and they probably didn't date from much before the seventeenth century. I met someone who made an aeolian harp in their garden shed. But let's cherish the idea of the wind blowing off the fabled Aegean Sea to set the strings of an aeolian harp vibrating and softly humming in some Arcadian grove.

The wind gusting down the Tottenham Court Road, sullied by dust and grime, rattled an old tin can.

*

A more boisterous wind, rich in ozone, blew straight off the Channel, over the Palace Pier and up the Race Course hill, snatching at the grey puffs of smoke from the crematorium chimney. We had just taken leave of my dad.

The Evil Eye revealed to me that Aleister Crowley had died in Hastings and been cremated in Brighton, where his friends and followers (including Kenneth?) had conducted a kind of Black Mass or other pagan ritual in the crematorium chapel. Was it the same one that I now stood outside? Aleister Crowley and my dad, both?

'Do what thou wilt shall be the whole of the law,' Crowley had declared. A bit too late for my dad. Short back and sides, a close shave every day, off to the office and back again, the shiny dark suit, or the grey shapeless trilby and grey shapeless trousers, dark blazer with a flap at the back, heavy black laced shoes with a strange little pattern stamped on the toe caps, perhaps the last vestiges of some conceit to be stamped into the ground, the navy-blue overcoat which he was always reluctant to take off on the rare occasions when we went visiting, as though it were his mantle of escape.

He'd tried escape in other ways. The unfinished model of Sir Francis Drake's ship *The Golden Hind*, a beautifully fashioned and painted hull and deck but bereft of masts and sails, that was never going to circumnavigate the world. The stamp collection with all those examples also from all around the world forever waiting to be sorted and mounted in two handsome red-bound albums. The violin that was never out of its case. At least on the golf course he could whack that little white ball as hard as he could up into the sky. But perhaps he was happiest at the far end of the garden or up on his allotment stoking a bonfire that allowed him to disappear in smoke.

Well, he'd done it at last. Aeolus was as good a god as any to carry him away in that same grey smoky stuff.

*

'What's your sun sign, Penny?'

'Pisces.'

'Ah, you swim both ways. Isn't that right?' I dropped the cannon ball back in place with a dull chunk. 'Are they real ones?'

'Oh yes, and some of them are inscribed with names.' They were too. Balaclava, Omdurman. The battle honours of Penny's great great grandfather, Major General Sir Somebody. We sat before his tomb, with that small pyramid of cannon balls in front of it. All around us an armada of other tombs and gravestones wallowed in the sea of tangled undergrowth, with their stone figureheads of angels looking piously heavenward or with heads bowed in sorrow and prayer, scarred and pitted by time. They may have retained some dignity in the peace and seclusion of a country churchyard. Here, in the middle of the great big city, such maudlin piety, the desire to be remembered, the hope of immortality, seemed just ludicrous and sad.

It was not the moment to say so. 'What about your dad?' I asked Penny.

'Oh, he was in the army too.'

'Another general?'

'Not quite. A colonel. We're a military family.'

I tried to match Penny's features against those of her illustrious ancestor, booted and spurred, the mutton chop whiskers, pillbox hat, gold braid. It wasn't easy.

I said, 'My granddad was a postman and a sergeant major in the territorials. Now look at us, sitting here, a couple of loners.'

Penny looked at me quickly and away again.

'That's a strange place,' I went on, returning to the house in Kensington.

'Why are you always going on about it?'

'Well it is, like something out of Spain or Morocco, and inside with those iron candelabra, they make me think of Dracula's castle.'

'There's only one candelabrum.'

'One's enough. And who is Princess Hapsetshut?'

'Hatshepsut -'

'Who is she anyway?'

'Look, can we talk about something else.'

'Some crackpot minor royal?'

'Oh!'

'Sorry. But come off it, Penny, you're worth more than messing about with all that indulgent and pretentious stuff. Woolly-minded. Now there's a good word for it.'

She looked at me for a moment, speechless, then turned and pointed. 'What's that over there?'

'The back of Stamford Bridge, Chelsea football ground.' I waved a hand about me. 'What a contrast, eh?'

At that moment a shadow fell upon us, as though one of those angels had finally managed to take off with a great flap of its stone wings. A big inky cloud had suddenly gathered itself out of the ether like some genie, expanding in all directions till it blotted out the sun. A rumble came from its blue-black belly, and with it that rare and passing fragrance as the first heavy raindrops soaked into warm dry ground. Then the belly burst.

'Over there!' I grabbed Penny's hand and we scrambled and half fell through the gaping window space of an abandoned chapel with no roof. 'Down here!' I jumped first into the empty vault half covered by large stone slabs. Penny followed. She fell on top of me, and that's how we stayed, give or take a garment or two, for quite some time, unmindful of the rain.

*

Had we, and was she, or had she still been, a virgin? No easy answers. Penny was a mystery in so many ways, slipping in and out of focus, more like a spirit than a real person. Look at the way she refused to let me see her home afterwards. We must both have been quite a sight, soaked and caked with mud. All the more reason to see her safely home. So who or what was she afraid of? Her dad, an officer and a gentleman, taking the horse whip to me or locking her in her room? I don't think she lived too far away, somewhere in the cosy hinterland between Chelsea and Fulham. That was another thing. I didn't have her address, I didn't even have her phone number. She'd called me every time. She called all the shots. Was it, was she, all a dream? Making love in a tomb in a thunderstorm?

'Just look at you!' Phyllis was out of her room in a flash.

'I know. Got caught in it.'

'Fell into it, more like!'

If only she knew. And if it hadn't been for those planks to stand on we might have been down there still. Six feet under.

Phyllis stopped abruptly with the castanets. 'There's your phone!'

I fumbled with my keys (God just suppose I'd lost them), shoved open the door, and made a dash for the instrument.

I snatched it up. 'Got home all right, then?' I panted.

'What on earth are you talking about?' It was Iris.

*

Dr Gutt, with monogrammed cuff links and pearl tie pin, sat behind the glass-topped acreage of his desk. On the wall behind him a powerful spotlight played directly upon us.

I scanned my copy of the Progress Meeting agenda. Item one. *Disorders of the Thyroid.*

'Disorders of Zer Zyroid,' Dr Gutt repeated out loud. 'Galley proofs due.'

His black horn-rimmed glasses, of a huge magnification, settled on Jock. 'Well, Mr Cairns.'

Jock paused and coughed. 'Any day now, sir.'

From the neck up, our managing director turned the colour of port wine. 'Any day, Mr Cairns!' Perhaps it was Jock's strabismus that maddened him, never quite knowing which eye to look at, or which was looking at him. 'Do we wait till doomsday! You will get back to the printers immediately after this meeting and give me a date!'

'Yes sir.'

The reflected light from the glasses described an arc across the ceiling and fell upon me. 'Haff you made a note of zat!'

Dr Gutt paused to take in air. 'Item two, *Medical Endoscopy.* Ready for setting.'

Ted's turn. 'Not quite, MG. It's a new technology and I have to keep checkin' up with the author. And markin' up the mathematics takes a lot of time.'

Dr Gutt nodded sympathetically. 'So when do you think you will be finished Mr Barlow?'

Ted pursed his lips. 'Another week should do it.'

'I hope so.'

Through the tall period windows of the Doctor's office plane trees, old and ample, quietly shed their leaves onto the flower beds and lawn of an elegant square. A hansom cab, or better still a landau, would have completed the picture.

We moved on to item three.

'*Forensic Medicine.* Advance copies due.'

The glasses settled once more on Jock and we waited breathlessly.

'Er, a slight hitch there, sir.'

'Hitch!' The port wine rose again.

'A spot of industrial action, sir.'

'Industrial action!' Anger notched up Dr Gutt's accent by several more degrees. 'If you mean zay are on strike, zen zair is no goddamdt action!'

'No sir.'

In the dead silence Dr Gutt breathed even more heavily. 'Ziss kind of nonsense has got to stop!' His voice suddenly snapped into a high falsetto. 'If we don't publish zer books we don't pay zer wages!' The gobstopper eyes fell back on me. 'Now you see what I am talking about. I hope you haff made a note of everything.'

Seated on the far side of his desk, Miss Perkins, of a certain age, legs crossed at the knees and ankles, head reverently bowed, had already taken down every grunt, snort and splutter.

*

I followed Jock back down to the basement. 'Why did you tell him they're on strike if they're not?'

'Because it's easier that way.'

'Easier than what?'

'The truth.'

'Which is?'

'We haven't paid their account.'

'Why not?'

'Ask his lordship.'

'Why don't you ask him?'

'Why don't you.'

I climbed back up the stone steps, past the old fuse box, sprouting wires like potato shoots. Across the hall Miss Perkins was back at her desk, seated like a concierge by the double doors to Dr Gutt's office.

'Don't forget to do an extra copy for me,' I said. She looked blank. 'The minutes of the meeting,' I prompted her.

Miss Perkins had to crank herself up before she spoke. 'The - minutes - of - '

'Oh, and he said you might type a few letters for me.'

Miss Perkins struggled with the enormity of my request. 'Who - said - ?'

I nodded at the double doors. 'His Nibs.'

'You - mean - '

'MG. Isn't that what Ted calls him? Think of sports cars.' I winked at her to devastating effect.

*

'Ziss kind of nonsense has got to stop!' The way Dr Gutt's voice rose to that high falsetto made me think of Klingsor, the black magician in Wagner's music drama *Parsifal*. I'd read that Klingsor castrated himself to channel his sexual drive into psychic power. Imagine. Ziss kind of nonsense has got to - wait for it - stop! It brought tears to the eyes. By the way, in the opera Klingsor was actually sung by a baritone. A bit of a cop out, I'd say.

Cop out or not, Klingsor himself was a fascinating character. He cropped up under various guises in the Arthurian legends, though Wagner's idea of him was probably inspired by a medieval king of Sicily, Landulf of Capua, who was said to have possessed the spear that pierced Christ's side on the Cross and had magic powers. Wagner's Klingsor had a magic spear, and a magic mirror, and with their aid he hoped to steal the Cup of the Holy Grail from the Knights who protected it. He also had the seductress Kundry in his power, to try and lure the knights into his magic garden where she corrupted them with her kiss.

Wagner was fascinated by magic and the supernatural, and he wasn't the only composer by a long chalk. Debussy wrote the music to a strange stage play, *The Martyrdom of Saint Sebastian*, which echoed much of the music of *Parsifal*, full of the same incense-laden ecstasy and doom. Debussy had a taste for the macabre as well. He planned to write an opera based on Edgar Allan Poe's novel of gothic decay and madness, *The Fall of the House of Usher*. Sadly he didn't get around to it except for a few fragments of the music. There was also Ravel with his piano pieces 'Le gibet' and 'Scarbo', a corpse swinging from a gallows to the lugubrious tolling of a bell, and a terrifying imp who appears out of the darkness before disappearing again into black night. And didn't someone write an opera called *Der Vampyr*?

Music and Magic. Come on, let's give it one more go.

*

In *The Fall of the House of Usher* the Lady Madeline has been entombed but escapes, bedraggled, deathly pale and mad. I don't think Phyllis had lost her marbles, but otherwise she looked pretty much like the Lady Madeline. She dabbed at her nose and eyes. 'It's my sinuses,' she snuffed. 'Watch.'

Phyllis blew her nose and a yellow mucus oozed from the corner of one eye. I thought of the cold custard poured over stewed prunes, with their slimy flesh and black skin that stuck to your teeth. 'Eat up, old man,' my dad used to say. 'They're good for you.'

Wiping her eye, Phyllis returned to her usual duties, shot into her room and out again with a parcel. 'This came for you.'

I weighed it in one hand. 'Not very heavy, is it? I mean, not for its size. I wonder what's inside.'

Phyllis hopped about, dabbing at her eyes. 'You know what's inside. Stop tormenting me!'

'I swear to you Phyllis, I haven't a clue.'

Nor had I, sitting up on my mattress, cutting the string and un-wrapping the brown paper. Inside was a shoe box, and inside that was a golliwog. He lay in state, arms down by his side. He was dressed in black and white check trousers, a ringmaster's red coat and tails, and he sported a polka-dot bow tie. The clothes were faded and worn, the big round whites of his eyes were not so white any more, the mop of black woolly hair was thinning out, while the lopsided mouth gave him all the pathos of a clown. He also had a note tied round his neck.

'My name is Hieronymous,' it said, 'and I want to be a friend for Blunderbuss.'

I lifted him out of the box and there was a newspaper cutting underneath. It announced the wedding of Miss Penelope Fortescue.

Fortescue! She was to be married to the Honourable - . I hardly noticed the fancy double-barrelled name, but putting two and two together I reckoned it must be her 'friend' whom she'd mentioned when we first met at the party and whose spectral identity had hovered around our conversations.

'Christ almighty Penny', I cried out loud, 'you don't love him, you love me!' An arranged marriage, it had to be. She'd been kept on ice, almost a prisoner, till their respective families agreed on a time and place. My God, that's how the old crowned heads of Europe used to carry on, with the fate of nations in their hands. I glanced again at the cutting. The wedding in some fashionable Chelsea church, bells, bridegrooms, confetti, grey toppers. Such funny things top hats, as Penny had also said on one occasion, a bit like wearing a chimney pot on your head.

I sat Hieronymous down by my pillow and put one of his arms round Blunderbuss. 'I reckon we're the three best mates she ever had,' I whispered to them.

*

And I'd dedicate my book to her. Hold on, hold on. I sat on the mattress, propped up by my pillows, with the two of them at my elbow, and my sheets of draft text all around me. There was my opening salvo, about music being magic, wired into the blood, witchdoctors and tribal instruments, and all that waffle. There was the stuff about the Harmony of the Spheres and Pythagoras, that I'd really sweated blood over. I picked up another sheet. Oh yes, astrology and what I thought that was all about, *The Planets Suite* and, as I had discovered, Constant Lambert's music for the ballet *Horoscope*. I picked up another sheet. The power of music to bring down the Walls of Jericho. A note about Heinrich Marschner and his opera *Der Vampyr*. Scriabin, of course.

So what did it all add up to? A sense of powerlessness overwhelmed me. This then is what happened when you tried to do something. At least when I tried to do something. An enormous weight descended upon me. Depression can exhaust you just as much as running a marathon. The difference is that with the one you move a lot and with the other you can hardly move at all.

*

'You look tired again this morning,' Phyllis greeted me.

The burden of depression had hardly shifted, but something else took my mind off it for the moment. It was an object almost as big as Phyllis herself and rather more beautiful. 'What's all this!'

'Just bought it, haven't I.' It was a Spanish guitar, the real thing, not some misshapen plastic electronic job.

'Where, may I ask?'

'Shop off the King's Road.'

I'd never thought of Phyllis going out at all, let alone to the King's Road. She could hardly have surprised me more if she'd said Peru.

'You didn't go like that, I hope.'

'Oh, do shut up.'

With the guitar now slung across her nightie, Phyllis struggled to find a chord, stretching her fingers wide over the fretboard and sticking out her tongue with the effort. Twang. Any chord on an acoustic guitar sounds magical, a breath of heat, a sense of vast and empty distance under the sun. Don Quixote country.

She stopped. Of course, the bloody post. She dashed back into her room, just avoiding a calamity with the guitar, and emerged with an armful of mail mostly in plain brown envelopes. 'Now what have you been up to!'

She might well ask. Some of the envelopes contained fairly innocent girlie magazines full of inflated boobs and bums like the ones on Ted's calendar. Then there were catalogues for sex aids and bondage, just as you'd imagine, with lots of black leather and metal spikes and whips. The black leather I could understand. So, I suppose, the whips. It was, after all, a very fine line between physical pleasure and pain, and if you were turned on enough you could easily make the cross-over. A lot of people evidently did. They liked handcuffs too. And what about those other catalogues showing pictures of tits with rings through the nipples, and that penis with a ring round its base, presumably to enhance erection (why did The Little Mermaid suddenly flicker through my mind). And before I forgot it, there was my order form for the *Karma Sutra*.

One more item on offer truly boggled the mind. It was an advert for a wooden box just large enough to hold the average sized man. According to the accompanying drawings he was first trussed up, blind-folded, gagged then locked inside. There was a button for him to press, that flashed an external light and rang a bell for someone to come and let him out when he'd had enough. Of what, for fuck's sake!

Hang on, what was this. I opened the last bulky package, and after a few seconds of gazing totally mystified at the article it contained the penny dropped. A sample dildo. It had to be. For the love of God, if I thought my dick looked remotely like that diseased and bloated rubber sausage I'd do a Klingsor and take an axe to it. I flushed the thing down the toilet and it kept floating back. Shoving it right round the bend, an arm in water up to the elbow, I heard Phyllis, still in the corridor, trying to pick out the notes and harmonies of 'The Foggy Foggy Dew' on her guitar. Someone else, I recalled, flushing the toilet one more time, sang that song to the accompaniment of a guitar.

*

It wasn't fog but a heavy curtain of suspended dust that a weak and weary shaft of sunlight cut through to fall exhausted upon one corner of the Progress Chart. This had belonged to Jock and was now propped against the empty fireplace in my office. It was a large peg-board, with a column provided down the left-hand side for the titles of individual books, while across the top, from left to right, were all the stages they had to go through from delivery of manuscript to publication. Pegs and strips of red ribbon were supposed to mark their progress.

You could, I reckoned, do a lot of other things with that Progress Chart. With a pair of dice you might turn it into a horse racing game, with the names of the runners down the left-hand side. Or with all those pegs you could play a giant game of solitaire.

My phone rang. It was MG. 'Will you come down!'

He had strewn over his desk a set of line drawings which I assumed were illustrations for *Disorders of the Thyroid.* One of the faces looked alarmingly like his own. Some of Percy's work no doubt.

Dr Gutt waved a manicured hand over them. 'Have you seen these?'

'No. Ted Barlow told me he had them and I asked Miss Perkins to let you see them straight away. We're behind schedule and I thought I'd try and speed things up a bit.'

In his agitation Dr Gutt may not have taken in exactly what I'd just told him. He fumbled once more with his intercom for the usual scapegoat. 'Will you come up?'

Jock arrived hastily stuffing his curly pipe into his jacket pocket.

'Haff you seen zees?' The accent thickened with the colour of Dr Gutt's face.

Jock skewered an eye onto the desktop. 'I don't think so, sir.'

'Sink!' The crimson flush deepened. 'I do not pay you to sink, Mr Cairns. I pay you to know!'

'Yes sir.'

Dr Gutt clumsily shuffled the drawings together. 'Take zem away!'

'What shall I do with them, sir?'

'Do you really want me to tell you, Mr Cairns!'

*

Jock's electric fire, one bar only, sizzled quietly and it was distinctly chilly in more ways than one.

I said, 'Sorry about that. I told him they'd come straight down from Ted.'

'Aye.'

'I'm only trying to speed things up, Jock.' I pointed to the drawings in question. 'A bit slap dash, aren't they.'

'Aye.'

'Percy's work?'

'Aye.'

'What do we do now?'

'Ask his lordship.' Jock retrieved the pipe from his pocket, sucked on it and resumed what he was doing. It involved a large square of white-coated cardboard, with sections of brightly coloured artwork, flowers and gabled windows and such like, divided by dotted lines and tabs.

I blew on my hands. 'What the hell's all that?'

'The Old Thatch.'

'Come again.'

'His country cottage.'

'Our lord and master's?'

'Aye.'

'What's that got to do with anything?'

'It's his Christmas card. You open it and it pops up.'

I had to laugh. 'Why don't you try the Tower next time and see how that pops up.' Outside on the pavement a dog cocked his hind leg and sprinkled the railings. 'By the way Jock, the Progress Chart. Why are the pegs in different colours?'

'Search me, laddie.'

*

Christmas! And while The Old Thatch might be popping up all over the Home Counties, I had Iris back on the phone. 'I can't just let the poor old bugger starve or freeze to death.' She spoke of Giles.

'I thought you'd divorced him.'

'Of course I have. That's not the point!'

So it was an errand of mercy that found us driving down the Kingston bypass on the very next Saturday morning. On our left a neon-lit Santa Claus with sledge and reindeer rode atop a petrol station. On our right, another car, with a fir tree strapped to its roof, suddenly cut across in front of us and raced away up the next exit slip. Hysteria crackled in the air.

I asked Iris, 'Where did you meet him?'

'Who?'

'Giles.'

'At drama school.'

'Drama school!'

'Don't sound so bloody flabbergasted!'

I smiled. 'You love that word, don't you?'

'What word?'

'Flabbergasted.'

'No I don't.'

'You said I was flabbergasted when you told me you'd worked for the BBC. That evening at the Music Club.'

'Did I?'

'Didn't you? Doesn't matter. By the way, how's Ingrid?'

'I don't know.'

'I thought you were friends.'

'Yes, but we're not that close. Why do you ask?'

'Nothing. What did you play at drama school? I can see you as Hedda Gabler.'

'Is that some sort of snide remark?'

'Not at all. Why did you give it up?'

'I wasn't good enough. Giles was the one with talent. At least he did have for a while.'

We picked up a bit of speed. 'Is it Esher we want?'

Iris gripped her sheet of scribbled directions. 'No, Oxshott. Keep going.'

'Aye, aye, skipper.'

Beyond the Hook Underpass the ribbon of houses and industrial estates finally ran out and there was a semblance of open country, if that's what you could call the neat and tidy patchwork of woods and fields spread out like a tablecloth.

Look to the sky for freedom. There were no walls or fences, no frontiers up there, only the marvellous alchemy of sunlight, air, temperature, humidity, atmospheric pressure and wind, to produce the endlessly changing drama of the skies, from breathless beauty to sullen gloom, always the same but always different, the stupendous backcloth to our lives. Right now the sky was the colour of a deep indigo bruise that weighed upon the land, heavy with intent.

'Leatherhead!' Iris pointed to the next turn-off. 'My God,' she cried, 'it's snowing!'

My God, so it was. Snow in our temperate climate, if and when it came, was always an event. Big wet flakes slid down the windscreen before they turned into a thick fluttering white veil that quickly settled on the road, making our wheel tracks trail snakily behind us, dark on fluffy white. Very large detached houses in a variety of styles, that in summer knew the soft plop of tennis balls and the plash of garden sprinklers, had quickly nestled behind a mantle of snow.

I waved a hand. 'There are your true tokens of wealth. Space and privacy. Just the little bit of it we can see right now, we must be talking in billions of pounds. And not just here. All over the country, bloody great houses and gardens, the most expensive cars, and yachts worth more thousands or millions. The mystery is, who are all these people? They can't all be oil magnates, city tycoons, pop stars or drug barons. What it boils down to is - '

'Stop!' Iris cried, taking another look at her directions.

We pulled up by a massive residence facing a split in the road and looking ready to collapse under its own weight of timbering. A notice on the big iron gates announced it as The Pines. A row of Scots pines were capped a snowy white against the leaden sky. We picked up a path by their side.

'It seems to take all the poison out of the world,' I said in a hushed voice. 'Not just the air but sound as well. Absorbs it like a poultice.'

'What are you on about now?'

'The snow. It seems almost a crime to tread on it. It's also like so much of life, isn't it? Beautiful for a little while before it turns to dirty grey slush.'

At the far end of the path was a field with what looked like a very large and lonely egg deposited in one corner. We crunched our way across to it and Iris banged on the door of a very small caravan. It rocked as Giles opened up, unshaven and holding onto those same corduroy trousers.

'Didn't you get my letter?'

He nodded in hazy recollection.

'Well, come on then.' Iris stamped her wellies in the snow. 'We haven't got all day.'

*

Giles slouched in the back of the car, long legs doubled up, with a disposal bag of empty bottles and greasy plates with whiskers of mould, and balancing a tin kettle on his knee. An odd smell, as of old and inflammable glue, filled the car.

'I'll bet you didn't know,' I said to break the gloomy silence, 'that Hindemith wrote an opera called *Sancta Susanna*, about a nun who gets the hots for the figure of Christ in the chapel. The Mother Superior reminds her that another nun who tore off her clothes in front of the same figure was bricked up in the chapel for her sins. But Susanna can't help it and does the same thing, then rips off the loin-cloth on the figure of Christ and an enormous spider falls on her and she goes bananas.'

'God almighty!' Iris cried. 'Is that what you're writing about?'

'No, but when you start doing a bit of research you pick up all kinds of stuff. What surprised me was Hindemith, you know, a bit of a stuffy old academic with his pipe and everything. Now if it had been Richard Strauss, after *Salome*.' I slammed on the brakes. 'Oh shit!'

Three lanes of solid traffic crawled up Roehampton Vale. 'Tell you what, we'll turn left at the lights, it'll probably be quicker in the end.'

Down Roehampton Lane, across the Upper Richmond Road and on down into Castlenau, where the traffic was stacking back from Hammersmith Bridge. So left turn into Lonsdale Road then Mortlake High Street into Clifford Avenue, over Chiswick Bridge, over the Hogarth Roundabout, and down onto the Great West Road where three lanes of traffic had ground to a halt.

'Fucking Christmas! Fucking snow!'

*

In the dim light of the room that Iris had found for Giles, there was a camp bed, a table, a chair, an earthenware sink with a cold tap, and a rusty gas ring by the grate. Iris, down on her knees, put a match to it and little blue flames sprouted from some of the holes. Down below, in the backyard of a shop, the last soggy patch of snow was melting fast among a clutter of cardboard boxes.

'There's a piece of music by Sibelius called *Tapiola*,' I said. 'In it Tapio, the spirit of the forests in Finnish mythology, appears out of a blizzard.' We warmed our hands on mugs of weak tea. 'When I was young, I thought it was called Tapioca. You know, like the milk pudding.'

Not a bleeding titter.

*

Rolls of fresh wallpaper, unopened pots of paint and plaster, brushes and a stepladder, filled Iris's hallway, while her living room remained almost as bare as a prison cell and a white shroud covered the grand piano. Still, it was a bit warmer in there, I'd grant her that. Slumped or dumped by the fireplace, in an old shirt several sizes too big for him, and a tie pulled into the tightest of knots round his neck, Giles appeared to have passed out in the unaccustomed heat. Clifford was there too, still growing by the looks of it and also attempting the beginnings of a beard. A jolly Boxing Day family reunion.

Crunching on a savoury twiglet, I asked Iris if she'd ever received one of those anonymous missives that looked as if it had been copied a thousand times and promised good luck if you sent out another dozen copies to friends or threatened the darkest doom if you didn't.

'You mean a chain letter.'

'Is that what they're called?'

'Yes.'

'And have you?'

'No.'

Who started such letters, and why? I could only think of post offices around the world who might benefit from them. At the same time they must upset a lot of gullible or vulnerable people. They were of evil intent. So who could have sent one to me?

I nodded towards the array of Christmas cards on Iris's mantlepiece. 'Did you have a card from Ingrid?'

'You're always asking about her.'

'Am I?'

'Yes. Fancy her, do you?'

I very nearly returned the savoury twiglet. 'No.'

*

Talking of Christmas cards, I'd had a surprise one from Adrian, and of a surprisingly exotic turn. It carried a picture taken from a 15th-century illuminated manuscript that I recognised as one of the illustrations from *The Evil Eye*. Two naked maidens, a blonde and a brunette - two of the sexiest witches you could ever wish to see, if that's what they were - stood back to back within the circle of the zodiac, with the various sun signs stuck over different parts of their anatomies. A scorpion, I noticed, covered the blonde's vagina. The sign of sensuality and passion, but not a nice place to get stung.

On the card Adrian told me he was now managing a bookshop in Hampstead and that card was selling like hot cakes. I'll bet it was.

In the New Year, he wrote, I must come up and meet Betty. His wife. Now there was a surprise!

*

'That's comin' on a treat.' Ted sat on the edge of my desk swinging his legs and pointed to a length of ribbon hanging loose from the Progress Chart.

'Who found him?' I asked.

'Fanny, when she looked in to say goodnight.' MG, dead at his desk from what looked like a massive stroke.

'Christ, that must have been a nasty shock for her.'

'Must 'ave nearly killed her too. Doted on him, she did. Stuck with him for over thirty years.'

'Was she married?'

'Professional virgin, mate. Lived at home with her invalid mother. All she ever asked of him was the two weeks off for Wimbledon.'

'The tennis.'

'Right.'

'Funny how women of her type, middle aged, middle class, go for tennis.'

'Yeah.'

'No other sport. Just tennis.'

'I know.' Ted expertly flicked his fag end into the empty fireplace.

We returned to the subject of MG. 'He's not still down there, is he?'

'Blimey, no! They came and fetched him last night, before rigor mortis set in.'

'Is that when the body stiffens up?'

'The limbs. Happens about three or four hours after death.'

Never what you might call a hive of activity, the building was now as silent as the grave. 'What about Fanny?' I asked. 'Miss Perkins?'

Ted shook his head. 'Finished, mate. Won't see her again.' He waved the book in his hand. 'I reckon this is what did it. Take a gander.'

It was the advance copy of *Forensic Medicine* that I'd been nagging Jock about. At least it was according to the paper jacket and the binding. Inside it was the contents for *Disorders of the Thyroid*. I flipped through the pages and stopped at the one containing the line drawing that I thought looked like MG himself and shouldn't have been there anyway. 'Christ!'

'That's what was on his desk.'

I pictured Dr Gutt, the offending volume open at that same page, slumped over the acreage of his desk, pop-eyed and purple of face, one hand and finger still reaching for Jock's button on his intercom. 'How the hell did this happen?'

Ted shrugged.

'But wouldn't Jock have seen it first?'

'My guess is it arrived just when he was packin' up, wanting to get back home to the bosom of his family. Probably didn't bother to look inside. Just handed it to Fanny on his way out and she took it straight in to his nibs.'

'Jock's married then.'

'Five kids.'

'Five!'

'Dark 'orse, mate.'

'Does he know?'

Ted nodded. 'Downstairs. Says he's still got some work to do.'

'What sort of a doctor was he, anyway?'

'Who are we talkin' about now?'

'MG.'

'Shrinker.' Ted grinned. 'Takes a nut to cure a nut. Mind you, he used to be good, I mean running this company. He had about twenty people in 'ere at its peak. But it's been going slowly down the pan for a long time.'

'So what do we do now?'

Ted shrugged. 'We've been in debt for years. Now he's gone I reckon we'll go into administration or liquidation. Sell off the remaining stock. And that'll be about it.'

'What about us?'

'Me? Right now I'm off.' Ted swung his legs off my desk and retrieved the book.

'By the way,' I asked, 'how did you get hold of it?'

Ted winked. 'Took it off his desk.' He patted it. 'Collector's item, mate.'

'Ted, I've been meaning to ask, what does the M stand for?'

But he was gone.

*

Standing outside in the Square and looking back across the road, I could make out Jock down in the basement behind the railings and the iron bars, still bent over his desk. After all the years of taking that stick from MG you'd think he'd be jumping for joy. You might also wonder why MG hadn't given Jock the push when the latter caused him so much grief. Perhaps in some odd way they'd grown to need each other. And now that one of them was gone the other felt suddenly lost. So sitting there at his desk and going through the motions, pretending that nothing had changed, may have been Jock's way of coping with the shock. He may not have wanted to go home either, to tell his family he was out of a job. I mean, if Ted was right, phrases like going into administration and words like liquidation sounded pretty terminal.

I raised my eyes to the tall elegant period windows of MG's office. In one respect it had been a privilege to have known him. With his accent (Hungarian or Viennese), immaculate old style suits, monogrammed cuff links, pearl tie pin, the pomade, and exuding a whiff of something between mothballs and camphor, he belonged to the world of Sigmund Freud and Carl Jung, of Gustav Mahler and Gustav Klimt. Well almost.

Through those windows I could see his floor-to-ceiling book-shelves. He had a dinky little set of spiral steps to reach the topmost shelf. And that reminded me of a story I'd read about the French composer Alkan. True or not, it said that he was found crushed to death in his gloomy Paris apartment by the bookshelves that had fallen on top of him, but with one arm and hand dramatically extended, clutching a copy of the esoteric Jewish *Talmud*. That's how MG should have gone, still clutching his copy of *Forensic Medicine*. In style.

*

'Stand clear of the gates,' cried the recorded voice in the lift at Goodge Street station. There was an edge of panic or despair to it, like the cry of a soul condemned to that black and gaping lift shaft till its term in purgatory was done.

'Stand clear of the gates!' It pursued us down the corridor, down the steps and along the length of the platform to the tunnel entrance, the Mouth of Hell, as portrayed in all those medieval carvings and paintings of the Last Judgement.

A stifled rumble came from deep within the Mouth, as all those other souls were digested in hell, and a belch of stale air blew scraps of litter between the tracks. The train rushed in, stopped with a squeal of brakes, the doors slid open, and onto the platform stepped a woman with nut brown hair parted at the crown of the head and falling in a half curl to brush the nape of the neck. I took in the shoes as well, black with solid heels, large buckles, and squared-off toes.

I only really saw her from the back, but my laser-like stare must have made her pause and turn her head. The face was quite different but almost as much of a shock as the one I had imagined. She resumed her walk down the platform and away. I felt a dizziness and heard a ringing in the ears. I sat down fast. Supposing it had been her, on a day off duty, doing a bit of shopping in Town. Or - God don't let me think of it - meeting someone else. The most beautiful but terrible visions came straight from hell.

Another train came in, and another. 'Stand clear of the gates!' echoed that desperate cry from afar.

*

'You're back early.' There was Phyllis cradling her guitar. It wasn't much after eleven, but I'd had more than enough for one day. 'You look like you've seen a ghost.'

She really was psychic with her deadly shafts of insight. But I wasn't going down the path of spectral phenomena. Stick to hard facts. 'The boss just died.'

'Oh me Gawd!' Phyllis strummed a chord. 'Sudden, was it?'

'A stroke.'

'Strokes don't always kill you. You can live for years after a stroke, can't speak or move your legs or someone has to wipe your arse for you.'

'You haven't had one, have you?'

'My mum did and I looked after her for five years. To tell the truth, I'd rather go quickly. Life's not that important anyway. Only idiots think it is. If you've got an ounce of intelligence it's hell a lot of the time.'

'I'm with you there.'

For a second time I'd stopped Phyllis in her tracks by taking her seriously and moreover by agreeing with her. She stood for a moment in stunned silence then strummed another chord. More or less recovered, she hopped across to the top of the stairs and leant over the rail as far as the guitar would allow.

'He's not still down there, is he?' she asked next.

My very words to Ted of not two hours ago. It really was uncanny.

'Roger. Just moved into the corner flat downstairs. That's his car outside. You must have seen it. The white BMW. Very flash. Jewish. His father's in the rag trade. Drove up like a maniac, not long after you'd left this morning. Already pissed out of his mind, must have been. Roaring his head off, slammed the front door, you know we're not supposed to do that, couldn't find the key to his flat and started shouting and cursing and kicking the door. You should have heard the language. Then fell asleep on the floor.'

'Well, he's not down there now. Anyway, why didn't you call the police?'

'They wouldn't come. Private property.'

'They would if he'd murdered you.'

'Oh thank you very much!' Phyllis tugged at a redundant bra and switched to more familiar ground. 'No post today. What about that other lot?'

'What other lot?'

'You know, all those packets.'

'This and that.'

'This and that,' she repeated scornfully. 'All right, what was in that other parcel?'

'What other parcel?'

'Stop playing with me! The box-shaped one.'

'Oh, that one. A golliwog.'

'I knew I shouldn't have asked.'

*

The name of Adrian's bookshop was Writer's Cramp.

'Isn't that,' I asked him, 'a bit like calling a pub The Brewer's Droop?'

'Brewer's Droop?' Adrian had loosened up quite a lot since I last saw him, away with the dark suit and collar and tie and on with a roll-neck pullover and gabardine slacks. All very Hampstead, but I think he still had some way to go.

'You know,' I explained, 'occupational hazard.' I tried a bit of Shakespeare, as far as I could remember it. 'It provokes the desire but takes away from the performance. Booze, Adrian. I'm not sure about provoking the desire but it certainly slows down the action, if you've had enough of it. Booze. The brewer's droop.'

'What's all that got to do with Writer's Cramp?'

'Well, another occupational hazard. When you've got it you can't write. At least, not with your hand.'

'Ah.'

Adrian's premises, at the corner of a romantic little alleyway by an old gas lamp, were certainly cramped in a more literal sense. Shelves bent under the weight of books, more were piled up in the window, on the counter, on the floor. A mobile dangled from the ceiling. You couldn't turn round without hitting something.

'How's business?' I asked.

'Booming! Our turnover's almost doubled since last year.'

'That's all those sexy cards you sell!'

'Sexy?'

'I'd say any picture of a couple of naked young women with signs of the zodiac stuck all over their privates was sexy enough. Got any Sylvia Bloom?'

Adrian smiled, which was a real treat. 'As a matter of fact, one or two titles.'

'I expect there's a lot of her old Omega stock still to sell off. To the woolly-minded, as Kenneth would say. Probably plenty of those round here.'

'Who?'

'The woolly-minded.'

'Huh.'

'You should get her up here for a signing session.'

'What!'

'With those thighs and those boobs she'd hardly get through the door.'

First the smile and now the laugh. Things were looking up. 'Right!' He clapped his hands. 'Come and meet Betty.'

*

Adrian had told me something of their situation over the phone. Going back a bit, Betty had some money of her own, and with him doing quite well, they'd lived comfortably in a large garden flat not so far away. Then Betty's funds ran low, Omega Books went to the wall, they'd had to leave the flat, putting most of the furniture in store, and now lived over the Bookshop. It had, said Adrian, all been a bit of a trauma for Betty. He came to the point. She had a sister who lived at Rottingdean, and since I told him I sometimes drove down to Brighton to see my mother perhaps next time I could go a little bit out of my way and give Betty a lift down to the coast. A couple of weeks' rest and sea air should do her a power of good. Naturally he'd pay for the petrol and any other expenses.

'This way.' Adrian ducked at the entrance to the narrow winding stairs to the upstairs rooms, or room. 'Mind your head.'

Betty was, let's say, matronly and sat in a chair looking almost as confined as an astronaut in a space capsule. They hadn't put quite enough furniture in store by the looks of things. Adrian stood by the top of the stairs and got a grip on the handle of a large suitcase.

'Ready darling?'

Betty in turn gripped the arms of the chair and struggled to her feet, catching at a lamp standard to stop it falling over.

Adrian led the way back downstairs, nearly coming to grief on account of the suitcase. In the shop he knocked over a pile of books and sent the mobile spinning. Outside, and with a great effort, he swung the suitcase into the boot of my little car.

Betty spoke at last in contralto tones. Had he got his migraine pills? She ran through quite a pharmaceutical list for both of them. My poor car rocked again as she got in.

Adrian bent down and pecked her on the cheek. 'Thanks a lot,' he said to me, waved and thumped on the roof. Take her away.

*

'It's fascinating, isn't it,' I said to Betty, 'entering or leaving a great city by car or train. In the centre you've got your famous landmarks or sites, Big Ben, Buckingham Palace, the Eiffel Tower, the Empire State Building, the icons that give the city its familiar face or character. But it's the rest I'm talking about. What you see from the car or train, like slicing through the city's sinews, its blood and guts, the pattern of the streets and roads, the taller buildings that give you a sense of distance and scale, the factories and depots, the criss-cross of railway lines and motorways. These are what make a city.'

Once we'd crossed Waterloo Bridge it was more like slicing our way through its dropsical belly, Lambeth, Brixton, Streatham, Thornton Heath, Croydon, Purley, Coulsdon and a thousand sets of traffic lights. At long long last the first hesitant signs of countryside, a horse in a field, an open slope of downland. Finally the motorway, and I knew how a greyhound feels when it's released from its trap.

I tried again with Betty. 'Talking of Writer's Cramp, have you ever had it? Very painful. The muscles in your hand just seize up and you can hardly hold a pen.'

She spoke at last. 'I can imagine.'

An aircraft arriving at Gatwick Airport swooped over us so low we could see the faces of passengers as they looked down at us in our little blue car, a moment's contact in the passing bubbles of our lives.

'Adrian was telling me about the grand piano you've had to put in store.'

'Yes.'

'What was it?'

'A Blüthner.'

'Wow. Did you play it a lot?'

'Now and then.'

'Who's your favourite composer?'

Betty shook her head.

'Not Bach or Beethoven or Mozart? What about Chopin? What about Debussy or Ravel?' It was one of Debussy's piano pieces, I told her, that first grabbed me as a child. *Jardins sous la pluie*. Standing there, looking out over our own rather drab and dull back garden, with the familiar backs of the houses opposite, there was a passage, a sequence of harmonies, that made the world suddenly tilt on its axis. 'I didn't know what hit me,' I said.

'I'm sure.'

'They're so rare, aren't they, those moments when the music catches you in just the right mood. It's like what you do to a fish, filleting, it opens you right down to the bone so that there's nothing left but the absolute truth, and you're weeping and laughing at the same time, such joy, such sorrow too, and afterwards you're just left speechless and gasping. You've had a glimpse of heaven, and it's almost too much.'

'Quite.'

The power and the magic of music, way beyond all words to describe. So what was I doing, trying to write about it? A sudden wave of despair nearly knocked me sideways and I swerved onto the hard shoulder of the motorway. Betty gripped her seat in terror.

Back in lane I resumed. 'Do you know Ravel's *Gaspard de la Nuit*? The title means something like Phantoms of the Night. They're piano pieces, must be fiendishly difficult. I love 'Le Gibet'. The way Ravel's chords capture the scene of a dark and stormy sunset as a corpse swings from the gallows to the tolling of a bell. Ravishing. They get the hairs standing up on the back of my neck.'

Still in shock, Betty clutched her knees.

'I expect you know they used to place the gallows at a crossroads to confuse the unquiet spirit of the dead person so that it would stay where it was and not cause any trouble. Dirty work at the crossroads, as they say.'

'Indeed,' she gasped.

'Incidentally, have you ever watched a pianist's hands on the keyboard? They look like the legs of a giant bird-eating spider, don't they? Imagine some giant arachnid playing Ravel!'

Now I really was talking crap.

*

Not before time the South Downs loomed up fast, bright and flaxen under a pearly sky. They weren't very high, nor of any great extent, no more than a faint smudge of yellow on most maps, but a world of their own, of long sweeping contours, lonely little dew ponds, chalky paths and flint walls, stubborn turf, wind-blown copses of hawthorn and stunted beech, everything scrubbed down and ready for the sea.

At Rottingdean it lapped hungrily against the sea wall, impatient to claw back the chalk-white cliffs it had cast up in the first place. At low tide you could see how it had succeeded, smoothing over the fallen chalk and dressing it from slippery green to a grey and black coat of limpets and barnacles to the iodine-brown wet seaweed wallowing at the water's edge, while in each little rock pool scarlet anemones and little darting crabs and shrimps waited for the first trickle of the turning tide.

'Turn left here,' said Betty, suddenly alert and with evident relief. We pulled up by her sister's cottage, its garden brushed with a light greyish coat of brine. Her suitcase nearly did for me as well.

Betty asked, 'Would you like a cup of tea?'

'No thanks,' I panted. 'I'd better be getting along.'

*

Mum's pale anxious face withdrew from the window as I came round the corner. She opened the front door before I was half way up the steps.

'I was beginning to wonder if anything had happened.'

'I thought I said I might be a bit later than usual.'

'Yes, but you never know these days.'

'What's so different about these days?'

'Well, you know what I mean.'

She'd sold the old house for a song. She didn't want to be greedy. Even then she could have moved into a decent little apartment off one of those broad avenues that ran down to the sea front at Hove. I'd have helped her. But without asking me she'd settled for a place on the main road, with a large black tree trunk and a bus stop right outside. Grubby lace curtains were strung across a length of wire, and a plant in a pot of rancid dust lolled half out of it, desperate for light and a breath of air.

'Shall I open the window a little bit?'

'Better not, dear. I might not be able to close it again.'

'I'll close it again before I go.'

'Leave it, dear.'

Mum had, of necessity, also sold off or given away many of her goods and chattels. Most of what remained stood around in that small dim room, much as the removal men must have dumped it, the flotsam of my childhood.

The sideboard and the wooden bowl on top of it, holding items of fruit that quietly shrank and rotted away. The upright piano, which had been such a rebuke to me when it came to practice, occasionally a source of excitement as I sought out strange harmonies. A complete and mostly unopened set of the novels of Charles Dickens, with their pictures of ladies in bonnets and voluminous skirts and of men in frock coats, top hats and boots that were my introduction to literature. The redundant fire screen with its embroidered picture of Ann Hathaway's cottage. The cake stand that, on the rare occasions my mum brought it out, had a habit of tipping the Swiss roll onto the floor. And leaning heavily forward on its chains, presiding gloomily over all, the large framed print of 'The Boyhood of Raleigh', so familiar in every tiny detail down to the beak of that toucan behind the old sea dog as he pointed out to sea. And don't forget the papier mâché missionary box in the form of a Zulu hut, into which mum sometimes dropped a coin. I don't remember anyone ever emptying the contents, but she was doing something for a good cause. The coins, now useless, were probably still inside.

I moved one chair to sit more comfortably in another. 'So how are you keeping then?'

'Oh, mustn't grumble. Touch wood. Things all right with you?'

'Fine thanks.'

'Praise be.'

Seated on a tiny folding chair she must have had as a child, mum gathered up the cake crumbs on her plate with her fingers, like the crumbs of her life.

The tea leaves in my mouth nearly made me gag. 'I'd better be off in a minute.'

The room had gone even darker. 'It does look like rain,' mum said, 'and you've got a long way to go.'

'Not really, but I've had a long day.'

'That's what I mean.'

At the door she clutched my hand, and in that action and in that look was so much unspoken love, so much anxiety, bewilderment and incomprehension. 'Give my love to Ann,' she said.

*

Soaking in a hot bath at the end of that long day, the soapy bubbles coalesced and split up, slowly spun and drifted around the surface of the water, like galaxies in space. Indeed you didn't have to stretch your imagination too far to think of them as such, composed as they were of billions of atoms and molecules in billions of soapy stars, each with its planetary system of electrons, protons and neutrons. And in the few seconds I lay there watching, a thousand million years had passed for them. All a matter of space and time.

I pulled out the bath plug with my big toe and now watched the water begin to circle and to dip around the plug hole until it formed a gurgling whirlpool. Reduced in scale, I'd soon be sucked down into that terrifying watery abyss. Incidentally, had I read or heard somewhere that in the northern and southern hemispheres the water circled either clockwise or anticlockwise, according to the Earth's rotation. And if you interrupted its flow and made it start to circle the other way, would you be defying the laws of physics?

Gusts of wild singing brought me back to a sterner reality. They rose up the bathroom ventilation duct from down below. They stopped. There was a sound of breaking glass, and a scream. We were beginning to get used to it. Roger entertaining a lady friend.

Sick, crazy people, psychopaths, schizoids, serial killers, paedophiles, alcoholics, junkies, don't usually come out of the woodwork shouting and screaming. You might be living with one cheek by jowl for years before you knew that anything was wrong, if you ever did.

Not so with Roger. Once he'd got half a bottle of brandy inside him he was literally raving mad. The trouble was that for the moment he was also as tough as an ox. We lived in fear at Linden Court of meeting him in his cups. And there didn't seem much hope of getting rid of him, not until, as I had suggested to Phyllis, he committed something akin to murder, so long as his father kept him in that flat.

I knew what I'd like to do. Strap him to a chair, pull back his head, wrench open his mouth, shove a funnel down his throat, and forcibly feed him with spoonfuls of hot treacle and boiling tots of rum (a change from the brandy) till his homicidal bloodshot eyes bulged and popped right out of his fat blotchy face and he burst asunder.

As a matter of fact, I knew of someone else who'd burst asunder a bit like that and who must have been just as terrifying in his later days. Henry VIII's funeral cortege from Hampton Court Palace to Windsor Castle had stopped overnight at Syon House. It was there, I believe, that the monarch's diseased and suppurating corpse blew up in its coffin. Next morning his faithful bloodhounds were found licking him off the walls and floor.

Not much left to bury after that, I'd have thought, reaching for a towel.

*

Roger and King Henry bursting asunder. 'Burst'. The word lodged in my mind, burst, birst, berst, and lost all meaning. A little phonetic bubble, ready to, well, burst. How frighteningly tenuous was our grip on language and perhaps our grip on consciousness itself. To forget the sense of a word was surely only a few steps away from forgetting who or where we were. God. There was another funny little word, waiting to float aimlessly around the mind and burst (birst, berst) like a bubble. Dog spelt backwards. Dog has a Message for all of us, as the Reverend Guinness might have said.

The big red letters W-O-O-L-W-O-R-T-H slipped past the window of the bus, to join Burst and God in my lexicon of the meaningless. Where the hell were we? Back in another part of that same dropsical limbo. Endless industrial estates, railway tracks from somewhere to nowhere, forlorn isolated pubs, second-hand car lots with tattered bunting, a prelude to the regimented ranks of semi-detacheds, marching shoulder to shoulder across a gently undulating and unresisting countryside as far as the eye could see and way beyond, leaving in their wake a beleaguered church with lych gate and churchyard where the dead might wait in vain for Judgement Day, a forsaken row of elm trees by the side of a muddy football field, a stream clogged with broken supermarket trolleys and the entrails of takeaway vindaloos.

The only takeaway in my young days was fish and chips wrapped in newspaper. No supermarkets either. Otherwise, the houses, the streets, looked much the same, give or take a garden gnome. That was the shock of it. Back to where I'd begun.

I sat in a daze while the bus joined a line of cars crawling up an incline behind a milk float. It finally pulled into the curb and stopped by a shop with a pile of wicker baskets out on the pavement and a window full of fish tanks. The lady giving me directions over the phone had said get off at the stop by the pet shop. Still in a daze, I hesitated. If I did get off would I ever be seen or heard of again.

Her mention of Sainsbury's helped. A comfortingly familiar name from the wider world. Keep on that side of the road, she said, and look for Sainsbury's, then turn down the alley by the side of it. At the far end was an electricity sub-station. Check. Attached to a steel gate was a dramatic sign, black on yellow, of a prostrate figure struck by a thunderbolt from Zeus. Danger high voltage. Next to it, she said, were their offices. By God, or by Dog, and so they were.

There was a notice on the reception desk by the door and a button. Please ring. 'Good afternoon.' A blonde-haired lady popped her head round the top of the stairs. 'Would you like to come up?' The voice on the phone made flesh.

*

'It's not quite Bloomsbury,' I admitted to Adrian. 'But they're smart modern offices, right next door to Sainsbury's, which is convenient, and children's books should be fun.'

'Sainsbury's,' Adrian sniffed. 'I didn't think you were the type for children's books.'

'I'm a child at heart, Adrian. Anyway, I'll have a go at anything.'

'By the way, is there something wrong with your phone?'

'Don't think so.'

'Well, you didn't answer for ages just now.'

'Oh that. I've been getting a lot of nuisance calls lately. Someone keeps ringing and then hanging up again. Or they wait till I answer and then don't say anything. So I wait till somebody speaks into the answerphone. Like you did. Then I pick it up.'

'Any idea who it is?'

'It may be a woman.'

'You and your women!'

'I don't have many women.'

'Well, you must have done something to upset this one.'

I winced at the memory of the flying hair brush. If it was her, of course. 'Anyway,' I replied, 'I bet you get some slick chicks in your bookshop. All those Hampstead types.'

Adrian snorted. 'They're married, most of them.'

'They're the best!'

'What?'

'Stuck at home all day, marriage in a rut, maybe drinking a bit too much and gagging for it.'

'It?'

'Come on, you know what. And there's you, running this bookshop, full of pictures of naked witches, a spare room upstairs and Betty out of the way. You're in clover. A different one each day.'

'What!'

In fact, was Betty the only woman he'd had? If he'd even had her. Hardly the type, I'd have thought, to ignite his or anybody else's passions. High time he broke loose. The

Playmates singles club for a start. He was as good as single. Okay, so most of the ladies were, shall we say, of a certain age. Not the ideal candidates to get the pulses racing or the dick to stir. But at least a change from Betty. And you never knew. I mean, that's where I met Penny.

I asked Adrian, 'Like to come to a party?'

'When?' he replied with alacrity. 'Where?'

*

Not quite Bloomsbury. Norman tucked the phone into his shoulder and deftly extracted a cigarette from his pack, stuck it between his teeth, flicked his lighter to it, and transferred it to his free hand.

'Yeah...Yeah,' he nodded absently to whoever was on the other end of the line. 'Yeah, I know.' He took a quick drag at the cigarette. 'Listen Bob, I'll...I'll...Yeah. Listen. I'll take another l-look at the figures and call you back. Sure... Sure. Ciao.'

Norman hung up, took another quick drag on his cigarette with a hiss through his teeth and returned to the matter in hand.

'I'm n-not sure about the hat, Cyril.'

Norman's hair was a fine comb-over. Cyril's was a silvery white. And he had his own special way with a fag, gripping it between amber-stained forefinger and thumb and dragging at it deeply while opening and closing each eye in turn. He'd seen the old world take a few turns.

'We could make it a bowler,' he said.

'Nobody wears b-bowler hats any more, Cyril.'

'They don't wear top hats either, except at funerals or at Ascot.'

'Who's talking about funerals, Cyril, or f-fucking Ascot!'

Norman and Cyril were an old team, almost like a variety act. They'd worked on the Whizz Kid Comic back in the good old Fleet Street days and they'd brought the name of Whizz Kid Books with them out there in the sticks.

The item under review was Croc the Doc, portrayed in vivid acrylic colours, grinning toothily back at us from the cork display board below the skylight in Norman's office. He reared up on his hind legs, improbably green tail stretched out behind him, with stethoscope, Gladstone bag and shiny black topper perched on his very low brow. A reptilian Dr Gutt.

Speaking of whom, and of medicine, I had an idea. 'How about giving him one of those mirror-type things that doctors strap round their heads when they want you to say aah and look down your throat.'

Norman frowned for a moment then with a broad smile he snapped his fingers. 'Hey, that might just work. Sarah!'

She popped her head round the door, as she'd popped it round the top of the stairs at me. 'Yes, Mr Kershaw.' A creamy contralto to Norman's light baritone.

'Could you get Hildie to come up for a m-moment.'

Through the neat square window of Norman's office, customers in Sainsbury's car park manoeuvred cars and trolleys in much the same silent, somnambulistic way as I'd watched the aircraft out of the window of Galaxy House. These were much friendlier.

A diffident tap on the door. Norman patted down his tie and brushed an invisible speck of ash from his sleeve. 'Come in and t-take a pew, Hildie.'

Fairly tall and very slim, she slid her tight blue jeans onto a chair and clasped one raised knee with long pale hands. Norman and Cyril took a drag together.

'Instead of the top hat, Hildie, we were thinking about one of those mirror things that doctors use.'

Hildie unclasped her hands and ran one of them through a head of fine auburn hair. 'How is it,' she asked in a soft beguiling accent, 'with such a mirror thing?' She half turned her head and smiled shyly at me.

'I'll show you,' Cyril said very smartly. He got up, crushed his cigarette out in Norman's ashtray, and unpinned Croc the Doc from the display board.

Hildie obediently followed him from the room.

*

She flashed through my mind and out again as a fuzz of light round the edge of the curtains proclaimed, in a disembodied sort of way, that somewhere out there it was another day, with people in the streets and traffic and life. I felt strangely light-headed, waiting for the baleful halo that was hovering somewhere above me to drop around my temples and turn into an iron vice.

So what time was it, what day was it, and where was I? Not alone. Someone stirred beside me. Last night's party! The Little Mermaid!

Why should I have been so surprised to meet her again? After all, in a great big city there were thousands of us, acting a bit like those free radicals that molecular scientists speak of, tiny particles drifting around looking for someone, something, to attach themselves to, dodging from one social group to the next, and by the laws of probability more than likely, sooner or later, to bump into each other again. Like me and The Little Mermaid. That look between us at Ingrid's soiree had been no casual glance. More a clash of nuclei. Now with smiles of instant recognition and hardly a word needing to be said, we took to the floor, hands and fingers entwined, cheek against cheek, groin soon beginning to press more urgently against groin, as we rocked gently to and fro, in or out of time to the music, in a perfect demonstration of that vertical expression of a horizontal desire.

Cathy, the name swam back into my mind. And what, if anything, had happened after I'd driven her back to her place and before we both passed out? She stirred again and rolled over, eyes still glued together but aware of me. She croaked, 'Are you awake?'

'Just about.'

'If you're going to the bathroom, could you get me a couple of aspirin?'

I threw back the sheet, not really dirty but not clean either, and somehow made it to my feet. Cathy's little black cat jumped off a chair and followed me, tail up. The bathroom smelt of its litter tray. The whole place did. Cathy's smalls hung over the bath on a rack. The lavatory bowl was a challenge to the strongest bleach on the market. Half-squeezed tubes, bottles, pads, cotton wool, creams and powders, hair curlers, tumbled out of the cabinet above the washbasin. Aspirins at last, and some water in her toothbrush mug.

Cathy struggled to raise herself on her elbows and unglued her eyes. 'Thanks,' she said, washing down a couple of pills.

I sat on the edge of the bed and took my turn with the aspirins. It was a large room with faded moulding round the ceiling and over the door that spoke of much better days.

'Last night,' I said. 'What happened?'

Cathy shook her head.

'Anyway, all a bit different from Ingrid's place.'

'Christ, yes!'

'Incidentally, how well do you know her?'

'Who?'

'Ingrid.'

'We worked together, ages ago. In a hospital.' Cathy managed a weak little smile. 'A loony bin, actually.'

'I thought she worked at the BBC.'

'I think that was afterwards.'

'You don't think she's a bit odd herself?'

'Aren't we all, sometimes?'

Fair point. I pulled on my trousers. 'Want the curtains drawn?'

'Not yet.'

I reached for a shoe. 'Anyhow, best not to tell her about us.'

'Who?'

'Ingrid.'

'Christ, no!'

I slipped into my other shoe. 'Thanks for everything. I'll call you.'

Cathy nodded and fell back on her pillow, and the little cat curled up at her feet.

*

'Eyes like piss holes in the snow,' Phyllis said, as I came wearily up the stairs. 'Where've you been this time!'

'Had to stay overnight with a friend.' Which was true enough. And staring back in the bathroom mirror at those two piss holes in the snow, I thanked God the fuzz hadn't been around. Not just last night either. I must still have been well over the limit. What a bloody fool.

Not that my occasional night on the tiles bore any comparison with him downstairs. Just about every morning the sound of Roger's convulsive pukes and groans greeted me from up the ventilation shaft. I was getting used to them by now. They sounded as though he were trying to turn himself inside out, indeed as though he were trying to expel some demon lodged deep in his gut. Once or twice, when I'd bumped into him at the front door or in the street, I thought I detected, behind the psychopathic stare, a look of terrible appeal. Save me, it seemed to say, I'm possessed.

Talking of demonic possession, if that's what it was, reminded me of something else I'd been reading up about. The Devil in Music, or Diabolus in Musica, as they called it in the Middle Ages. This was a special chord of two notes, or the interval between them, and it was loaded with significance.

You began with the chord of the open fifth as, for example, from note C up to note G on the white keys of the piano. Such a chord has a satisfying sound, as of something perfect in itself, humming away like those wonderful celestial harmonies. Pythagoras also loved the open fifth because of its arithmetical proportions within the scale. But if you lowered the top note of that chord by half a tone, as from note G down to the adjoining black note of F sharp, it sounded as though you'd bent or twisted the perfect fifth out of shape, perverted or corrupted it. That was the chord of the diminished fifth or, looked at the other way round, the augmented fourth.

Allowing for changes in tone and tuning since medieval times, that was also Diabolus in Musica. Another name for it was the tritone, because it spanned three whole tones up the scale. An unholy trinity, you might say, and the Church had banned its use in religious music for hundreds of years.

By the nineteenth century, however, it was a source of fascination for composers. Diabolism was all the rage in books and paintings, and Romantic composers also loved to send a shiver down their listeners' spines with their use of the tritone. Liszt, Mussorgsky, and most famously Saint-Saëns in his *Danse Macabre*, each made use of it. And, of course, we always came back to Scriabin. He strung three tritones together to produce what he called his 'Mystic Chord'. Yes, and look what happened to him when he took a shave.

Well, I thought, still staring bleary-eyed at the mirror, it was a Sunday, and I didn't need to. And later on, when I'd had a kip, and if I felt up to it, I'd try my hand at getting something down about Diabolus in Musica.

I thought I'd given up.

*

'Diabolus in Musica.' Adrian mulled the title over. 'The Devil in Music.'

'That's right.'

'Is this to do with the book you mentioned that time to me and Brewster?'

'Yes. Music and Magic. Remember?' I tried to imitate Kenneth's brusk and breezy voice. 'Not my line of country.'

'I know,' Adrian said again. 'It was all or nothing with Brewster.'

He reclined on the floor of the room over the shop, where there was just enough space by the window. I sat in Betty's old chair, my feet propped against a lamp stand that in turn leaned back against the wall.

Adrian asked, 'Do you mean music as a form of magic?'

'Yes, like all those ideas about a divine or magical Harmony of the Spheres. Or, you could look at it the other way round and think of all the pieces of music inspired by some magical theme.'

118

'Such as?'

'Well, for starters, all the compositions inspired by the story of Faust and his pact with the Devil. I mean, that's pretty magical. Black magic.'

Adrian yawned and smiled. 'Like Sylvia Bloom famously said.'

'Yes, I know. Poor old Kenneth and his magic wand.'

Adrian sat up with a jolt. 'His magic wand?'

'That and his talismans.'

'His talismans!'

'Just souvenirs he got from Aleister Crowley.'

'How do you know all this?'

'That day I went down to collect *The Evil Eye*. He showed them to me.'

'Good God. So she was right!'

'Sylvia Bloom?'

'Yes!'

I shook my head. 'Taking an interest in something isn't the same thing as practising it. Anyway, getting back to what I was saying, Schumann, Liszt, Wagner, Berlioz, Gounod, they all had a go at Faust. Then there's *Night on the Bare Mountain*, *Swan Lake*, *Lohengrin*, *Parsifal*, *The Firebird*. Lots and lots more. They're all to do with witches and magicians and ghosts.'

'A big subject,' Adrian said a little more calmly.

'Yeah, and I'm beginning to think too bloody big for me. You have all these wonderful ideas buzzing round in your head, but they're like clouds in the sky, beautiful from a distance, but when you try to bring them down to earth, get some of them down on paper, they just evaporate. I don't know if that makes any sense.'

Adrian nodded thoughtfully, leaned half over and gripped the litre bottle of Valpolicella. He changed the subject. 'I should have done this ages ago.'

'What, just lying back and letting it all hang out.'

'That's right!' He gazed up at the ceiling and went off on another tack. 'You were well away with that woman at the party.'

'Someone I'd met before and we just sort of clicked.'

'I could see that!'

'I'm sorry. I left you rather in the lurch.'

Adrian sighed and repeated, 'You and your women. Who was she anyway?'

'Her name's Cathy. She lives somewhere in Notting Hill. A nurse. You know what they're like.'

Well, some of them anyhow, and I don't suppose he did. 'Actually I think it was a case of the Brewer's Droop with her. Remember, we talked about that.'

Something else I suddenly remembered. I'd staggered off that Sunday morning without her address or phone number. She didn't have mine either. The demon drink. I reached for the Valpolicella.

'By the way, I reckon Cindy could be a bit of a goer after a couple of drinks. If you like big girls. You know who I think fancied her?'

Adrian raised his head off the floor. 'Who?'

'Sylvia Bloom again.'

'What!'

'A rogue lesbian if ever I saw one.'

'What!'

'I'll swear to it. Think of the two of them together, on the job. All sweat, big tits and fat heaving thighs.'

'God!'

'And a dildo.'

'What's that?'

'A rubber penis, or a plastic one. I think they strap it on to do the business.'

'Christ!'

'Well, what else would they do with it?'

We considered the options, while the old lamp outside in the alley came on with a soft and mellow light.

'How's Betty, by the way?'

'Fine.'

'Still down at Rottingdean?'

'That's right.'

'She told me about her piano.'

'I know, and it's costing me a bomb.'

'How so?'

'Keeping it in store.'

'Yes, of course. Wait a minute. I've got this friend. She's already got a grand piano, but she might have room for yours as well. It's quite a big house.'

'She!' Adrian scoffed. 'Another of your women!'

'No, no, not like that. I've known Iris for years. We're old friends. She's in publishing too. You two might get on.'

I slid my feet off the lamp stand that wobbled before righting itself. 'Anyway, time I was making tracks.'

We both wobbled a bit going down those stairs.

'Wait a minute.' In the shop Adrian reached under the counter for a brown paper package. 'Don't go without this.'

'What is it?'

'You'll see.' He opened the shop door with a merry little tinkle. 'I think it's your sort of thing. There's so much Saturn in it.'

Would that be to do with the big summer storm cloud rising up in the background of the painting Adrian had just given me? It was another watercolour in a simple gilded frame, and you could almost see the artist's brush twisting, stirring with relish the powdery dark pigment into the paper, making the cloud seem to grow and billow as you looked, just like the one that caught Penny and me in front of her ancestor's tomb. Or perhaps Saturn lurked in the ruins of the castle, whose broken walls and turrets rose above the encircling mantle of trees and creeper, with a glimpse of a moat. But it wasn't a sad or a menacing scene, not with the small party of sightseers in the foreground, frock coats and crinolines and a little white dog, and a picnic lunch spread out on the grass. The sun would always shine upon them, capping the cloud a creamy white, touching the stone ramparts with gold and holding the scene in silent rapture.

On the subject of ruins, what was their huge attraction? The word said it all, decayed, tumbledown, useless. And yet they were seen in such a romantic, even a sacred light, Stonehenge, the Pyramids, the Parthenon, the Roman Coliseum, Fountains Abbey. Perhaps it was simply the hallowing effect of time. In my picture those towers and turrets were built for pouring boiling pitch or red-hot sand onto those beneath to send them screaming with agony into what would have been the cesspool of the moat. Look at them now, the mellow stonework sprouting grass and herbs, the haunt of rooks and jackdaws, while water-lilies spread across the moat.

*

'Adrian,' I said to him over the phone. 'This painting is a little masterpiece. I mean a really fine piece of work. It reminds me of Samuel Palmer, if I've got the name right. There's something quite mystical about it.'

'Samuel Palmer?'

'He was a quite famous English watercolour artist, wasn't he? A bit like William Blake. I think he lived at about the same time.'

'So you like it?'

'My God, Adrian, it's so good it ought to be in an art gallery where lots of people can see it. And it must be worth a bob or two. Where did you get hold of it?'

'It's a family heirloom.'

'And you've given it to me! I mean, what have I done to deserve it!'

'Quite a lot, my friend.'

So I'd helped him dump Betty, got him half pissed, told him about dildos. Maybe that was a lot.

*

Steady rain beat a gentle tattoo on the skylight in Norman's office. Beneath it his rubber plant shone unnaturally bright from whatever it was that Sarah rubbed into its great fleshy bottle-green leaves.

Norman reached for his pack of cigarettes. 'They all smell like bloody soap to me, Cyril.' I'm surprised he could smell anything with his fags.

He had on his desk several large rolls of specially treated paper, fresh from the printers. On them were sample images of flowers and fruits, and when you rubbed them with a finger they were supposed to exude the appropriate scent. Scratch and sniff were the latest novelty in children's books. 'What would we c-call them, anyway?'

Cyril dragged pensively on his own coffin nail. 'Fragrance Books?'

'Too poncey.'

'Smellies.'

'Bugger off, Cyril!'

Norman let the pages roll up again and we returned to the problem of Croc the Doc, back on the display board with what now looked like a miner's lamp strapped round his head.

'Doesn't look m-much like a mirror to me,' Norman observed gloomily.

I said, 'Shouldn't it be slightly concave and have a hole in the middle?'

'A hole?' Cyril's lips squeaked when he took another drag, a faintly melancholy sound for a wet afternoon.

'Yes, for the doctor to look through when he's examining your throat.'

Norman brightened and snapped his fingers. 'That's just the kind of thing kids p-pick up on. Can we g-get Hildie to have another go.'

Cyril squeaked again, got wearily to his feet, unpinned Croc the Doc from the display board one more time, rolled him up, and left the room for Hildie's little downstairs studio.

'Smellies!' Norman grinned and shook his head, pushed aside the printer's rolls of paper and turned his attention to my proposal for a new picture book series.

Music and Magic, the Harmony of the Spheres, Scriabin, Klingsor, and all the rest of that stuff was fast becoming so much wreckage, but maybe I could still salvage something from it. So how about an illustrated children's series on stories from music, with a magical touch? There were plenty of good ones to choose from. For a start I'd listed *Hansel and Gretel*, *The Sorcerer's Apprentice*, *Swan Lake*, *The Flying Dutchman*, *Scheherazade*, *The Firebird* and *Der Freischütz*. They'd all fit the bill perfectly. Then we could add a bit about the life and times of the composer, about things like ballet and opera, then tell the story with pictures. Aimed at, say, the 8 to 12 years age group. Educational with a light and breezy touch.

Norman listened to my chat as he skimmed through the list. He looked up. 'What's this last one?'

'*Der Freischütz*. It's a German opera.'

'Crikey! What's it mean?'

'Something like The Marksman. It's a good story.'

Max, I summarised, was a young woodsman in love with Agathe, daughter of the local governor or prince. But she was to be married to whoever won the forthcoming shooting contest. In his desire to win the contest Max is persuaded by his sinister friend Kaspar to make a pact with the Devil, or as he's called in the opera, Samiel the Black Huntsman. They go to a grim and frightening place called The Wolf's Glen, where Kaspar summons Samiel, who agrees to cast for Max seven magic silver bullets. On the day of the contest six of these bullets all hit the target. Max is declared the winner and gains Agathe's hand in marriage.

Norman listened intently, the smoke from his cigarette rising in a thin grey plume. At the end of my account he asked, 'I thought you said there were seven bullets?'

'There are, and when Max fires his seventh bullet it hits Kaspar who's been watching from the battlements of the castle and he falls dead to the ground. Samiel had reserved it for him because he'd tried to wriggle his way out of his own pact with the Devil by bringing in Max. So justice is done and all ends happily ever after!'

Norman took a satisfying drag. 'I like it!'

'I thought we might call it 'Max and the Magic Bullets'.

'Great!'

The rain had stopped, the skylight sparkled, and the rubber plant positively glowed.

'Stories from Music.' Norman savoured the idea. 'I've been thinking for a long time we should move a b-bit upmarket! Raise our profile, so to speak! Good stories with an educational slant as well.'

He grabbed a sheet of paper and a pencil. 'Let's say A4 format, text on one side, illustration on the facing page, say twenty-three spreads for the text, one spread for the intro, then the title pages, thirty-two spreads in all. Why don't you draft out a specimen text, say around a hundred and fifty words per spread, for Max and the M-Magic Bullets. Then maybe we can get Hildie to sketch out a couple of spreads. See how they look.'

Bringing Hildie in sounded good to me.

*

Not far away, somewhere the other side of Sainsbury's car park, late each afternoon, the Convent of the Little Sisters of the Poor rang the Angelus on their bell. It somehow spoke for the name of their order, a sad and plaintive clang.

Not like the great bells of Christendom. Traditionally cast in earthen pits with much heat and sweat, they were brought forth from the womb of Mother Earth, blessed by a priest and named, as at a baptism, and often inscribed with strange and mystic ciphers. Then they were hauled by ropes or chains, a dangerous and sometimes fatal job, high into a tower. And there they hung, inert and silent, until they began to swing from

126

side to side, slowly at first, then with greater momentum, higher and higher, while their clapper gave tongue to their myriad harmonics, a hum of growing intensity that echoed the Harmony of the Spheres. Great bells, some poet said, excavated heaven. And if anything spoke with the tongues of angels it was the bells.

Look and listen to the way they fascinated composers. There was Puccini fussing over the exact pitch and sequence of the bells of Rome, as they chime the hour just before dawn at the opening of the last act of *Tosca*. Mussorgsky bringing in the joyous clamour of the Kremlin bells for the coronation scene in *Boris Godunov*. The chime of Wagner's deep and solemn bells or gongs descending into the Hall of the Grail in *Parsifal*.

Composers loved to imitate them too. Berlioz and his very clever off-key sound of a solo horn like the tolling of the bell that accompanies the pilgrims in his Symphony *Harold in Italy*. Bizet also using horns to represent a chime of bells in his incidental music to the play 'L'Arlesienne'. Ravel's doleful chime in his piano piece 'Le Gibet', as I'd described it to Betty, and his other piano piece, 'La Vallee des Cloches'. Britten's stunning use of horns to evoke church bells ringing on a bright Sunday morning in one of the 'Sea Interludes' from his opera *Peter Grimes*. And before I forgot, there was Debussy's piano piece 'Cloches á travers les feuilles', an evocation of bells sounding through the trees, and his piano prelude, 'La Cathedrale engloutie', evoking the tolling of bells of a sunken cathedral rising up from the sea.

Talking of submerged cathedrals and bells, the sound of one under the sea must be awesome. Sounds travelled faster and with greater volume through water, especially salt water, didn't they? So the sound of a bell must come at you with greater intensity, like being embraced by a vocalising octopus.

A tarantula playing Ravel. A vocalising octopus. How easy it was to go mad. How tough it was to write anything, 'Max and the Magic Bullets,' just as much as anything else. Two or maybe three hours later, at whatever god-forsaken time it was, I suddenly stopped and the mind went blank. I stared out of the window into the empty night for a few more minutes, then tried to stand up and nearly fell over again, half-drunk with fatigue. Great fun, this writing lark.

*

Cyril came out of Hildie's studio. 'I could fuck the arse off that,' he said, with an engaging candour.

She had swapped her jeans for a black skirt and knee-length lilac socks.

'Cyril is such a sweet old man,' she said to me, dabbing a spot more yellow on the beak of PC Penguin Pete, one of Croc the Doc's pals in *The Zany Zoo Book*.

'Snow on the roof, but a fire in the hearth,' I replied.

'It is not snowing, I think?'

'No, it's not snowing, Hildie.' I looked at my watch. 'Come on. It's nearly six o clock.'

'So we go now?'

She washed her brushes in the jar of water, raised herself from her high stool with a soft puff of sound from the padded seat, and reached for her light plastic mac and beret from the hook by the door. Almost Lili Marlene.

Out in the alley, Norman's car was parked by the side of the building. However late in the evening, it was always there, while a light still shone from his office window.

I pointed to it and said, 'Catching up on his paper work with Sarah.'

'Oh ja, I am sure!' Hildie chuckled solemnly.

'Lovely evening, anyway.'

It was, when you raised your eyes from the backyard clutter belonging to the parade of shops the other side of Sainsbury's, the battered dustbins, scattered litter, broken fences, the weary tufts of grass that survived the dog turds and the cats' pee. Feathery white clouds trailed high across a sky of deepening blue.

'Bloody cold up there,' I said. 'I think those feathery kinds of cloud are formed from ice crystals. High winds up there as well. They usually mean a change in the weather.'

'Ja, I think so.'

'Clouds have such beautiful names, don't they, Hildie. Those ones are called cirrus. Then there's cumulus, banks of flowery white cloud, nimbus, dark clouds bringing rain, cumulonimbus, great dramatic piles of cloud bringing more rain and thunderstorms, and stratus, cloud banks quite low in the sky. I could spend my whole life watching clouds. Just water vapour, but they make our planet. Not that most people care. You see them walking along with their eyes glued to the ground. They only think it's a fine day when there are no clouds at all. Minds as vacant as the sky.'

'Ja, and I think that makes you sad.'

'Yes it does, Hildie. There's so much beauty out there, so much to wonder at, so much to feel and to think about, and you can see in most people's faces, hear it in their voices and what they say, that they're dead to it all, and that sometimes makes me feel so alone. Or does it just make me a stuffed-up elitist, a toffee-nosed snob?'

Hildie paused in her step. 'I am sorry. How is it with the toffee?'

'Very bad for the teeth,' I said.

*

We passed the pet shop and the Aphrodite kebab house and reached The Galleon, a road house anchored solidly in brick and cement with a pub sign fit for a biscuit tin. It was still quite early in the evening and the place was half empty, the row of fruit machines flashing and flickering in an aimless frenzy. I carried our drinks to a corner table, away from the juke box, just in case.

'So here's the deal, Hildie. Norman's keen on this new series, Stories From Music, you know, the plots of operas, ballets, that sort of thing. I write the texts, you do the illustrations, lots of big ones. How's that!'

She nervously fingered her glass. 'I don't know so much about music.'

'You don't need to know a note of music, Hildie. They're simply stories for you to illustrate. We're starting off with *Der Freischütz*.'

Hildie looked faintly alarmed.

'You should know what that means. You're German, aren't you?'

'Neh, neh, I am Dutch.'

'Okay, Dutch.' Our conversation strayed. 'So what brought you to this neck of the woods?'

'I am sorry?'

'What brought you way out here, off the beaten track?'

Hildie puffed out her pale cheeks. 'Oh, it is a long story. You don't want to know.'

'Yes I do.'

She took a sip from her glass and fixed me with her big green eyes. 'Oh well, I came over here from Holland to study art for a little time. Then one day I met this bloke and he said all sorts of things.'

'What sorts of things?'

'That he worked in advertising and that I had much talent and so on and he could find me lots of work. He did find me a little bit. Then we got married and we moved to this house not so far away, out here in the woods, as you say. Then he went off with someone else and left me alone in the house.'

'He walked out on you.'

'Ja, I suppose that's how you would say it.'

'Why would anyone want to walk out on you, Hildie!'

She blushed suddenly and deeply, looked up quickly and down again at her glass. 'I am very lucky to have this job, to have some money.'

'What about maintenance?'

'I don't know so much about that.'

'Well, you ought to. He should be made to pay something towards your upkeep. He's still married to you, isn't he?'

'Neh neh, we got a divorce.'

'You might still get something out of him.'

'Ach, I don't care. Let him go.' Hildie shrugged and fixed me again with her big green eyes. 'I am glad. He was not so good at anything.'

*

Der Freischütz was a landmark in the history of opera, notably of Romantic opera, especially the scene at the Wolf's Glen, as Samiel casts the magic bullets, counting out each one to a rising chorus of demons and monsters. This, I thought, was the scene to get Hildie's pulses rising, bring another flush to her cheeks, a flash of fire to her eyes. I returned to the text I'd drafted the other night. It was flat and dead upon the page. Let's start again.

The phone rang. Adrian sounded excited. 'Listen, you remember giving me Iris's phone number.'

I didn't. What had we talked about while the Valpolicella went down? Kenneth and his magical paraphernalia. Me and Cathy. Sylvia and Cindy on the job. Oh God yes, Betty and her Blüthner and the cost of keeping it in store. And me opening my big mouth about Iris and her piano and her big house with lots of space. 'Did I?'

'Yes, and I've been in touch.'

'With Iris?'

'Who else! And we hit it off just like that!' I could almost see Adrian smacking the fist of one hand into the palm of the other. But he'd hardly begun. Iris was going to take the piano, at least for the time being, which shook me for a start. Then things went really wild. The lease on Writer's Cramp was running out and he had to find somewhere else to live so Iris was going to take him on as a lodger. How was he going to compare with Sam in bed? Hold on, when Adrian had settled in they might start a literary agency. He'd get it going, from her place, and if things went well, she might join him full time!

How about Sylvia Bloom as their first client, I thought crazily, while an old nonsense rhyme my dad used to recite to me as a child suddenly came back into my head.

'With a grand piano on his back,
Upstairs he tried to run.
He stood on a stair that wasn't there,
And his day's work was done.'

I now saw Adrian as a demented Franz Liszt, all flowing white hair and coat tails, charging up Iris's stairs with Betty's piano on his back and ending up squashed flat beneath the instrument, hands and feet sticking out from under it, broken keys and twisted wires everywhere. Great stuff for the bizarre and sometimes violent world of *Struwwelpeter*.

That, of course, was the secret of so much classic children's literature (think also of the Brothers Grimm), the element of violence which children loved. It was a part of growing up. Wham! Pow! Splat! Come to think of it, that might be the trouble with *The Zany Zoo Book*. Not enough blood and guts. We could get Croc the Doc to saw off somebody's leg, have PC Penguin Pete beat the living daylights out of The Wicked Weasel with his truncheon. Get Hildie to paint in a lot of dizzy stars and a big red lump on The Wicked Weasel's head. I mean, Norman would know all about that sort of stuff from his days at Whizz Kid comics. Maybe I'd have a word with him.

'Sorry Adrian, what did you just say?'

'When her birthday comes round we're planning a bit of a do.'

'Who's birthday?'

'Iris's of course!'

*

Sycamore seeds have those lovely 'wings' that spin round as they descend from the tree. Alas there were none to be seen in Sycamore Road. Instead, the pavements were lined with what might once have been plane trees, hacked down to leafless knobs like cudgels, provided perhaps by a thoughtful council for those who wished to end it all. The more each house and garden tried to look different the more they all looked the same.

Except for one. On what had once been a patch of lawn there stood a large whitewashed motor tyre with some wet sand at the bottom of it. The remnants of crazy paving led to the front door. I hopped along it and pressed the door bell, which answered with a stutter. Hildie, back in her jeans, opened up.

'I love those dandelions,' I said.

'Ja, I am so ashamed. It is all such a mess.'

'No, no, I mean it, Hildie, about the dandelions, they're exquisite little sunbursts, miracles of creation. Bloody silly people call them weeds just because they're doing their own thing.'

'Ja, I think maybe that is true.'

She led me into her front room, which couldn't have changed much since the day it was built. The bow-fronted windows were garlanded with little boiled sweets of coloured glass. A smoked-glass bowl hung by chains from the centre of the ceiling, marked by radiating grey streaks from dust and from those coal fires that had once burned smokily in the grate. Hildie had scattered rugs of various hues and patterns over the floorboards that didn't quite cover them. She invited me to sit in a giant cushion filled with beads, which was like falling into a quicksand. The more you struggled the deeper you sank in.

She sat on a wobbly chair, a bit like me and Penny in reverse. 'I think you are not so happy with the cushion,' she said.

'I'm fine, Hildie.' I handed up to her my bottle of wine before it swallowed me completely.

She left the room and came back with two glasses and a very old and obstinate corkscrew.

'I am sorry,' she said.

134

'Stop apologising, Hildie.' With a desperate tug I pulled out the cork. 'I'm blissfully happy.' I poured out some wine and raised my glass. 'Here's to us!'

She sipped her wine and crossed her long slim legs. 'I think maybe you want to get me drunk.'

'No, Hildie. I want us to work.'

With a crunch of those beads I handed up to her my draft text for the Wolf's Glen scene for 'Max and the Magic Bullets'.

She leaned forward in her chair, frowning with concentration, and I tried to follow her eyes as they scanned my words.

'Max and Kaspar finally reached the Wolf's Glen after a long walk through the dark forest. It was a place of rock and stone and littered with the bones of animals that the wolves had left behind. Max shivered. It was icy cold and he was scared stiff. But Kaspar stood boldly in the middle of the Glen. 'Oh mighty Samiel,' he cried. 'I summon thee to my aid!' A wind began to blow, faster and faster, like a whirlwind. Hideous demons and monsters suddenly appeared out of it, screaming and shrieking. And in their midst stood the terrifying figure of Samiel, the Black Huntsman.'

She finished reading and a large shaggy dog padded into the room. He ponged a bit and dribbled. Hildie looked up.

'I am sorry. Mengelberg has got out of the kitchen. I think you are not so fond of dogs.'

'It's small yappy dogs I can't stand, Hildie. Lapdogs, like Yorkshire terriers, with their strangled little voices and long red curly tongues, and if you look under that fringe of hair they've got black beady eyes and a fixed grin, like a spider.'

'My God, you think so!'

'My grandmother had a Yorkshire terrier called Pickles. He used to wank himself in his basket.'

'Please,' asked Hildie. 'What is wank?'

*

One afternoon each month granny invited her two surviving friends round for tea. We were back again with *Struwwelpeter*. Preserved in mothballs and Eau-de-Cologne, Miss Dwyer was large, with a big hairy mole on her chin and a charcoal soft moustache, and she wore antique black leather boots buttoned half way up the calves of her legs that creaked as she moved. Miss Clifton was tiny and blue-veined. She sported a murderous hat pin, a veil that always got tangled up with her hair, and a little velvet band round her throat that rose and fell about her dewlap as she spoke or swallowed.

For the occasion granny laid out her best bone china, blue and silver sugar bowl and tongs, a small white jar of Gentleman's Relish, and triangles of trimmed white bread and butter, hardly more substantial than the Host. These were reverently partaken, to the tinkle of cups and spoons and murmured conversation that rose and fell like a liturgy. And all the while there came a gentle creak of wickerwork, as Pickles in his basket, front paws gripping his blanket, little shiny red prick exposed, strove for a climax never quite attained.

*

In the deep shade of the hall, granny also had the picture of a forlorn and solitary figure, blindfolded and hunched atop a grey and misty globe, plucking at the one remaining string of an old wooden lyre. The picture was called 'Hope'.

136

Substitute the lyre for her guitar and Phyllis could have posed for that painting. She hopped out of her room. 'Now where've you been?' she asked.

It was nearly eleven o clock at night. Time had gone fast with Hildie.

'Working, Phyllis.'

'Pull the other leg.'

'I'm telling you. Discussing artwork for a book.'

'Oh yeah? Seen Roger?'

'Not recently, thank God.'

'He came in this morning, after you'd gone. Covered in bandages.'

'Like a mummy?'

'No, not all over, stupid. Just his head.'

'More like a turban.'

'Sort of, with a red spot on top.'

'Like Jupiter's big red spot.'

'Oh, for God's sake. Blood! Been in a fight. Hit over the head.'

'How do you know that, Phyllis?'

'Well, he must have been. We had the police round here later on asking questions.'

'I thought you said they wouldn't come in here.'

'Oh, do leave off.'

'So what did they ask you?'

'If I'd seen anything.'

'And had you?'

'Only what I've just told you.'

'All right, so did they arrest him?'

'He'd gone out again.'

'They should have dragged him away and strung him up by the balls.'

'Oh, very nice, I'm sure!' Phyllis paused in her doorway and turned round again. 'You're not in any trouble are you?'

'Not more than usual. Why?'

'That envelope.'

'Which one, Phyllis. I've had so many lately, haven't I.'

'Oh, do shut up. The one that came yesterday.'

It was a small buff envelope marked On Her Majesty's Service, and it was true that Her Majesty's Service nearly always meant bad news or trouble for someone else.

'Oh, that one. As a matter of fact it was a summons.'

'Oh me Gawd!'

'That's right.'

'What for?'

'Jury service.'

Phyllis's face took a couple of turns. 'They've never asked me!' She was hotly indignant about it.

'The Old Bailey.' I rubbed it in. 'Only the best for me.'

'When?'

I tapped my nose. 'When Justice calls.'

*

Hildie had called her old dog after Willem Mengelberg, the famous Dutch conductor.

'You said you didn't know anything about music.' I sank once more into the quicksand of her bead cushion.

'Me, I don't. But my grandfather used to go to the Concertgebouw in Amsterdam and there he told me he saw Mengelberg. I think one time he also saw Rachmaninov.'

'Did he!' I told Hildie Rachmaninov had very long fingers that could stretch across more notes on the keyboard than almost anybody else, which is why a lot of other pianists find his music so difficult to play, because he wrote most of it for himself. 'Mind you,' I added, 'a lot of other composers did that.'

Hildie sat attentively in her chair as though I was giving her a lecture, so I thought I might as well carry on.

'Rachmaninov belonged to the next generation of Russian composers after Tchaikovsky. He came from a fairly well-off, land-owning family in old Tsarist Russia, and when the Bolshevik Revolution broke out in 1917 he thought he'd better get out. So he and his wife and two young daughters escaped through Finland and into Sweden on a open sledge in the middle of the winter. Think what that must have been like for them. Huddled together on a sledge with all that ice and snow, and dark nearly all the time.'

'My God.'

'I know, and he never went back home again. He was desperately homesick for the rest of his life but he never returned to what was then the Soviet Union. His music sounds deeply nostalgic for old Mother Russia, the great rolling plains and forests and the chanting of the Orthodox Church, although in fact he wrote most of it before he went into exile. Ended up in Beverly Hills, California.'

Hildie shifted in her chair. 'How do you know so much?'

'God.' I put my hands to my cranium. 'You make me sound so big headed, Hildie. It's just that I listen to a lot of music and then I want to learn more about it. Anyway, going back to Rachmaninov, not all his music is so full of nostalgia. He wrote one piece called *The Isle of the Dead*.'

It was, I told her, inspired by a painting of that name, of a boatman rowing a tall white shrouded figure across a mirror-calm lake or sea to an island with a grove of cypress trees like tall black candles and tombs cut into the rock.

Hildie's eyes opened wide.

'You can hear it in the music, the slow sombre rhythm of the boatman's oars, and as the piece builds up to a big climax Rachmaninov quotes from the old plainsong chant for the Dies Irae, the Day of Wrath. That must be the same as the Day of Judgement, when the Bible says we're all going to be summoned back from the dead to answer to God or Christ for our sins, and either go to heaven or to hell.'

Wallowing in the bean cushion I struggled once more with that corkscrew.

'Do you believe in a Judgement Day, Hildie? You know, the way it's depicted in all those medieval stone carvings in churches and cathedrals, and in all those paintings and murals. The good ones who are going to heaven on one side, and on the other side the Devil with his horns and a tail and his pitchfork, herding the damned into the gaping mouth of hell.'

'Ja, I have seen many of those pictures.'

'Think what it must have been like to live in the Middle Ages and really believe in hell and damnation. That's how the Church kept its power, through fear, not through love. Mind you, I'll bet people still sinned just as much. Drink and sex. You can't change human nature.'

'Ja, I think that also.'

'Incidentally,' I ploughed on, 'if the Church still truly believes in a Judgement Day, how come it allows cremations. I mean, if you're reduced to a small heap of ashes you can't rise again from the grave, can you? But it's all still there, in the Bible and in the Creed. I know, I recited it enough times in church. From thence he shall come to judge the quick and the dead. I believe in the resurrection of the body and life everlasting. Mind-boggling stuff, but does anybody in their right mind really and truly still believe it in this day and age?'

Mengelberg raised his shaggy old head from his paws.

I admitted that some of those old prayers in the Anglican prayer book were very fine, probably going back to Tudor times, and some of those old psalm tunes were pretty good too, strong, simple harmonies to appeal to everybody.

I crunched around some more in the cushion. 'God Hildie, talk about verbal diarrhea. Please tell me to shut up.'

'Neh, neh. It is good that you talk. You think seriously about these things. You should write them down.'

Ha bloody ha. Where had I heard that before? I clapped my hands. 'Anyway, enough is more than enough. How are you getting on with Max at the Wolf's Glen?'

Hildie looked ruefully down at me. 'It is not so easy.'

'Nothing worthwhile is easy, Hildie,' I said, finally drawing that cork with a satisfying pop. 'And starting is always the hardest part.'

'Ja,' she said, 'that I know.'

*

Iris's front door bell did not stutter. It chimed ding dong, ding dong. A stranger opened up. No, it was Clifford. He'd grown so much taller, he'd let his sandy hair grow too, all curly round the back and sides, and he sported a copper ring in one ear lobe.

'Hi.' He stood paralysed for a few seconds as though not sure what to do next till I took a step forward and he hopped aside to let me pass. I was going to ask him why a ring in only one ear, but we reached the kitchen first, where Iris was down on her hands and knees with a bucket and cloth, mopping something off the floor.

I smiled and waved my bottle. 'Happy birthday!'

'Yes, yes, thank you. Just don't step in here!'

I carried my birthday gift on into the living room which finally had some paper on the walls, and the covers were off the furniture, but it still didn't feel much like home. Giles sat by the empty fireplace, with the same oversize tartan shirt pulled tight round the neck by the same ill-matched tie. He looked fast asleep.

Stepping through the French windows, someone had also made an attempt to clear up the garden and cut the grass. The broken swing remained.

Adrian was poking and blowing at a barbecue.

'No smoke without fire!' I quipped. 'Bit chilly for this, isn't it?'

'It was all right while the sun was out.' He tossed more kerosene onto the smouldering lumps of charcoal and almost disappeared from view, like my dad with his bonfires.

Iris bawled from within, 'Shut those bloody windows or you'll stink the whole place out!'

With the French windows firmly shut, we sat in the living room and ate sausages, from near cinder black to near raw pink, with garlic bread, limp lettuce leaves, and a glass of something or other, but not from my bottle. Giles had roused himself and wouldn't look me in the eye.

I couldn't keep it off Iris's grand piano in one corner of the room. I should think it would take the rest of her life to pay for that on what she called the old drip feed, as black and shiny and sleek as a Rolls Royce, and probably almost as expensive. It was also crying out to be played, to be loved.

'Do you mind if I have a go?' I asked, of no one in particular, and no one said a word.

I'd half prepared for the moment. A single chord had been haunting me. I'd looked it up in a copy of the score, figured out the notes and how to place my fingers on the keyboard.

Now I walked over to the instrument, raised the lid on the strings and on the keyboard, releasing the smell of brand new felt and dampers, then sat down on the stool and placed my fingers on what I hoped were the right notes, before letting them sink into the keys.

The chord rang out, like the deep dark chime of a great and gilded clock. It filled the room, it transfixed the view through the windows, from garden to chimney pots, to the thickening shroud of sky. It tilted the Earth once more upon its axis, that deep purple chord. Synaesthesia was the word, the effect of all the senses rolled into one.

The sound of it decayed and died. Silence in music is every bit as important as sound.

*

Adrian gathered up what was left of the sausages and garlic bread and I followed him into the kitchen. 'What's up?'

'We had a bit of a row.'

'Before I arrived?'

'Yes.'

I pointed to the stain still on the kitchen floor. 'Did that have anything to do with it?'

'No, no.' Adrian shook his head. 'Clifford dropped a sauce bottle or something.'

'So?'

'That fellow Giles drank my bottle of Champagne. Every drop of it. Then she goes and defends him.'

'He must have had most of my bottle too. You can see the state he's in. I suppose Iris feels protective. He's like a child to her now.'

'We're all children to her.' Adrian finished the washing up. 'Must wear these you see,' he added, peeling off the rubber gloves. 'Fancy a walk?'

Coming out of the front door I caught a glimpse of Betty's piano in the empty front room, propped against the wall with its legs off and half under wraps, abandoned. Poor Betty. Poor Adrian. He'd just complained about being treated as a child, but perhaps deep down that's what he wanted. He fell for motherly or for domineering types. How would he have got on with Ingrid? What a fascinating but hair raising thought.

We stepped into the street and I asked Adrian, 'Had it off with her, have you?'

'Had it off?'

'Come on Adrian, shagged Iris.'

'Good God, no!' A bit too oedipal perhaps in view of what I'd just been thinking.

'Okay, so what about this literary agency idea?'

Adrian snorted bitterly and mentally wrung his hands. Evidently no go there either. 'Where do I keep going wrong?'

'Timing, Adrian. Well, that's not all of it, of course. I mean physical appearance, personality, experience, things like that are important. But however talented you are, however good at what you do, however hard you strive, I reckon that at the end of the day you've got to meet the right people in the right place at the right time, otherwise you're fucked.'

Adrian nodded gloomily.

'I'm not just talking about work and career. Everything. You meet the one person who seems made for you, personality, voice, looks, sex, everything, but if it's at the wrong time it ends up tearing you apart. Actually so much of life ends in bloody tears.'

'Sounds as if you're speaking from personal experience.'

'What else, Adrian. I've left a trail of wreckage in my wake, misery for me, misery for others. I'm not looking for excuses, it's just bad timing more than half the time. But I'll tell you something else. When one thing goes wrong, everything goes wrong.'

We waited by the traffic lights at a junction with the busy Upper Richmond Road. 'Incidentally,' I added, 'have you ever read the Book of Ecclesiastes?'

'In the Bible?'

'Yes. I dipped into it recently and it says much the same thing, about luck and timing and the rest of it. Time and chance govern all, it says. We're born, we live, we make it or we don't, and that's an end to it. Good book, Ecclesiastes.'

'I didn't know you were religious.'

'I'm not. Not in the conventional sense anyhow. And it seems to me that a lot of Ecclesiastes isn't specifically religious either. It's just good plain common sense. Or wisdom, if you want to use a more high-flown word.'

We crossed the road onto Barnes Common, and Adrian took a deep breath. 'I've got other problems,' he suddenly blurted out.

I wondered what was coming next.

'It's to do with words. I have to keep counting them, the number of words in a sentence, in a paragraph, on a page. Sometimes I even count the letters in a word. It's crippling.'

I should think it bloody well was, in a publisher and a bookseller. Perhaps it had something to do with the demise of Omega Books. Too fussy, too obsessed, couldn't make up his mind. 'Is that what they call an obsessive compulsive disorder?'

'Something like that.'

'Bruckner, the composer, had the same kind of thing. If he started counting the number of paving stones on a street and thought he'd missed one out he'd have to go back and start again. He'd even try and count the number of leaves on a tree. And in his music he fussed obsessively over the number of bars in a certain passage, or the number of notes in a melody, stuff like that.'

'Does he come into your book?'

'No. There's nothing magical or occult about his music as far as I'm concerned. It's all long weighty symphonies and Te Deums and things.'

'So how's it going?'

'My book? It isn't. I've just about given up.'

'You seem to take things quite calmly.'

'You think so, Adrian? My moods go up and down like a yo-yo, almost from minute to minute. Everything gets to me.'

'You hide it well.'

My turn to be a trifle bitter. 'I just brood and fester.'

*

Before we knew it we'd stumbled into a graveyard of sorts. There was no church or chapel, not even a set of railings or other boundary to mark the site, just a cluster of tombstones around a stone pillar amidst thickets of laurel and yew. A nomadic graveyard, a circus of the dead. Come back next week and it might have picked up its headstones, wrapped up its coffins and bones, and moved on in a ghostly cortege.

In the sudden muffled quiet and stillness, Adrian asked, 'What was that chord you played just now?'

'Wonderful, isn't it. From one of Debussy's piano preludes, *Feuilles mortes*. Dead Leaves.' I shuffled a few of them around with my feet. 'Dead leaves, or like looking down into a pool of still deep black water.'

'God, there's so much Saturn in you!'

'So you say, Adrian.'

'I must do your horoscope.'

'Since we're on the subject I'll tell you one thing that bothers me. All those astrological constellations, Aries, Taurus, Sagittarius, and the rest of them, you could make almost anything out of the stars they're based on, couldn't you? It's like joining up the dots when most of the dots are missing. Talk about pie in the sky!'

Adrian sighed. 'There's so much more to it than that.'

'I know, I know. Just raising a point.'

Back on open ground, the wind had picked up, carrying with it a soft drizzle. It also lifted a lock of Adrian's hair, exposing the high dome of his forehead. He was going bald. You suddenly noticed these things in others, and in yourself. The ageing process was not a steady one. It was like walking down an irregular flight of steps to the grave. You might linger on one step for a while, looking, feeling, behaving much the same. Then you took the next step down, and you'd grown older overnight. Iris had lately grown heavier round the jowls, thicker round the hips. I was losing teeth. You looked at other people and thought, my God, what's happened to them, then realised they were probably thinking exactly the same thing about you.

Waiting to cross back over the road I said to Adrian, 'I've got a bit of the obsessive compulsion thing myself. I have to keep checking things all the time, like turning off the cooker or taps or a light, especially when I'm going out. Sometimes I'll get half way down the stairs and have to go back, a bit like Bruckner, to fiddle with a switch or a door handle. Or when I'm out I'll keep checking to see if I've got my keys or my wallet.'

'That's a very common neurosis.'

'Maybe, but it shows something's a bit out of kilter, doesn't it? I'll tell you something else, I can't stand pictures that aren't straight on a wall. What does that mean, I wonder?'

'You're a perfectionist.'

'That I like!'

Back across the Upper Richmond Road, Adrian asked, as Betty had done, 'Like a cup of tea?'

I pulled up my collar against the thickening drizzle. 'No thanks, Adrian, I'll be getting back to my little pad.'

He heaved the deepest sigh yet. 'God, how I envy you.'

Adrian may have said that, but none of us, no matter who, and no matter how bad, wretched or desperate our situation, can ever really conceive of being anybody else. A life sentence and no mistake.

*

My thoughts drifted back to the wreckage of Music and Magic. What or who could I blame for that? Bad timing, bad luck, my bloody cusp? Or Penny for putting me up to it in the first place? Listen, don't cast around for excuses. It was just an impossible subject, or I wasn't able to make anything of it. I'd tried and failed, and that same dead weight of fatigue that I'd felt before descended again. Let me get back to my little pad, as I'd said to Adrian, draw down the sea green blinds upon the damp and dismal end to the day and lie down in gloomy solitude.

'Have you heard?' Phyllis demanded before I'd reached the top of the stairs. She hopped from one foot to the other, the closest I'd yet seen her get to being beside herself. She raised her voice. 'I said, have you heard?'

'Heard what?'

'He's dead!'

'Who's dead?'

'Oh for God's sake, Roger! Wrapped his car round a lamp post. Earlier today. Took nearly an hour to cut him free.'

'How do you know?'

'It was on the news.'

'Well, all I can say is hooray!'

'Ooh!' Phyllis was shocked. 'That's a wicked thing to say!'

'No it's not. He was a drunken maniac and he could have killed the lot of us at any time.'

'Doesn't matter. You shouldn't speak ill of the dead.'

'Bugger the living and the dead!'

I slammed my door behind me and instantly felt terrible. The silence out in the hall was palpable. Poor Phyllis. She couldn't help being a pain in the ass sometimes. That was no way to treat her.

And that was something else I had to live with, the way I felt so bloody guilty all the time, about so many things. That was just as crippling as your OCD, or whatever they called it.

*

Hildie balanced her plate on her lap. I put mine on the floor, where I could just reach it from the depths of the cushion.

I held up a scrap of chicken bone. 'Poor wretched little creature, packed in with thousands of others just like it, pumped full of antibiotics, wings clipped, killed without ever seeing the blessed light of day, feathers plucked while its body was still warm. If we had kept it in a small yard or back garden where it could scratch happily around that creature would have come to know us, even to love us in its own way, and we'd have loved it in return.'

Hildie shook her head. 'I don't like to think about those things.'

'That's the trouble, none of us do Hildie, if we bother to think at all. But I'll tell you what I think, or what I hate. People talking all the time about humans and animals. We're all animals, Hildie, all part of the tree of life, all connected with each other, humans, apes, tigers, eagles, spiders, deep-sea squids. It's appalling arrogance, isn't it, to believe, assume, that we're somehow separate from all the rest of the animal kingdom? And there's more to it than that. If we don't have respect for the rest of the living world we can have no love or respect for ourselves.'

I could have rambled on, getting more and more incoherent, about vivisection, about the morality of kindness and cruelty in our relationships, the place of religion in it all, and on and on. But I reckoned Hildie had had enough when she began to gather up the remains of our sad and simple meal and carry them out to the kitchen, with Mengelberg padding behind her.

That was something else. When people did talk of a love of animals they usually meant just dogs and cats. But was that love or mere self-indulgence? Weren't they simply using those creatures to compensate for some lack in themselves and by so doing taking away the animal's natural dignity? Look at poor old Mengelberg. Yes, but enough was enough.

I called out, 'Can I help?'

'Neh, neh.'

*

After what seemed a very long time, Hildie returned with a large artist's portfolio. She went down on her knees, slowly undid the faded pink ribbon and began to take out some of her old drawings and paintings.

'My God!' I cried. I couldn't help myself.

She instantly stiffened. 'They are so bad?'

'No Hildie, they're good. They're very good. It's just that some of the objects you've drawn are sort of imprinted on my retina.'

'How is that?'

'They're stuck like photographs in my mind. Like that one, the interior of St Peter's, Rome.' There was the angel, and that hand of a pontiff raised in benediction. 'I've drawn that too.'

'My God, so you are an artist also!'

'No, well maybe, if I'd stuck at it. No, I drew them while I was in hospital. I was given an old copy of the *National Geographic* Magazine and copied them out. Therapy. That's all.'

The cavernous old ward, the smell of disinfectant and cabbage water, the anodyne chimes of an ice cream van patrolling the streets outside, while I struggled with the barley sugar columns of Bernini's Baldacchino.

'So you were in hospital? You were very sick?'

Why, for the hundredth time, didn't I keep my big mouth shut? 'All psychosomatic, Hildie.'

'My God, what is that?'

I waded in deeper still. 'It's when something that's worrying or distressing you makes you physically ill. Mind over matter.'

'So what was it that - '

I clapped my hands. 'No more questions, Hildie. Come on. What else have we got here?'

Just as slowly and hesitantly she handed down to me her first pencil roughs for 'Max and the Magic Bullets'. The one for the Wolf's Glen was about as chilling as a pantomime stage set for Aladdin, and Samiel could have been Aladdin himself. He wouldn't say boo to a goose.

There she sat all day, in her little studio by the alleyway, with scalpel and glue pot and paints, punctuating the hour with the tinkle of her brushes in the water jar, removing Croc the Doc's top hat, messing with Penguin Pete's truncheon, while her talents drained away.

'Not bad for a start,' I said. Hildie dropped her head as though it had been axed. 'The technique's good.'

'Ach, bloody technique!' That rare flush returned to her pale face, and with an even rarer passion she kicked and scattered her work with her bare feet.

I grabbed her hands. 'Listen, Hildie, I know all about despair. You work so hard at something, and it's like trying to pin a butterfly to a page and still keep it alive. Or you work at something and you're so pleased with it for a little while, like a beautiful pebble all wet and shining from the sea, till next day, when it's dry, it's lost all its sparkle and its colour.'

'My God.' Tears suddenly flooded those big green eyes. 'That is true.'

'Come on, Hildie, don't cry.'

'I am drunk, that is all.'

'Actually, like you said the other day, it's sometimes good to cry.'

'Did I?'

'I'm sure you did.'

'Ja, and maybe you should try it too.'

'I have, my darling Hildie, believe me I have.' I stroked her silky auburn hair, gripped those slender shoulder blades, felt the thumping of her heart.

She raised her head and the air whistled softly through the narrow bridge of her nose. She wiped a hand over her eyes and the same hand over mine.

'Mengelberg is getting a nuisance.' She cleared her throat. 'I think he goes in the kitchen.' She got up from her knees. 'And I clean my silly face.'

'It's the most beautiful face in the world, Hildie.'

She blew her nose and struggled with a smile. 'Don't go away, please.'

*

Saturday morning after Friday night and I crept up the stairs of Linden Court. Weary yes, but not hungover this time, no eyes like piss holes in the snow, no shadow of shame or guilt. I might look Phyllis straight in the face and tell her it had been beautiful. I reached the top of the stairs. So where was she? Now I thought of it, I hadn't seen anything of her for several days. Then I remembered. Oh God, that business about bloody Roger and his bloody death.

I tapped on her door. Nobody much likes apologising, to admit that they've been in the wrong, that they've lied, deceived, or behaved badly in some way. But it's a bit like throwing up, you feel so much better afterwards. I tapped again, a little louder. A pause, a shuffle from within, and she opened the door by half an inch.

'Phyllis, I'm so sorry about the other day. I was a bit depressed, a bit down in the dumps, but that was no excuse for the way I carried on, swearing and slamming my door like that. Can you forgive me?'

Now didn't that make me feel much better!

She opened her door another half inch. 'I thought you hated me.'

'Never in a million years, Phyllis! If that was the case why would I be apologising now?'

She emerged, the nightie, the slippers, but something was missing.

'Where's the guitar?'

'Sold it, didn't I.'

'Why?'

'Dunno.'

'But you were getting really good at it.'

'I thought you didn't care.'

'Listen, if I didn't care - ' All the same, she could be so damned maddening sometimes.

Phyllis sniffed and wiped an eye. 'Are you coming to the funeral?'

'Whose funeral?'

'Roger's, of course.'

God give me strength!

*

I had this brilliant idea for another children's picture book. I'd come across this story of two nineteenth-century American palaeontologists who were also bitter academic rivals and who travelled out to places like Colorado and Wyoming in a race to discover fossil bones of some of the most famous dinosaurs, Triceratops, Stegosaurus, Diplodocus, Brontosaurus, Tyrannosaurus Rex. Their story had it all, dinosaurs (kids couldn't get enough of them), mad professors (I could pile that on a bit), and the great days of the Wild West, the Indian Wars, the building of the first railroads, the lot. I even had a title, 'Battle of the Bone Men'. There was the educational side too, geography, natural history, Darwin and evolution. With a good racy text and illustrations to match, it had to be another winner.

'D-don't really sing, do they.' Norman took a drag at his cigarette and brought me swiftly back to matters in hand.

Hildie's new pencil roughs were a shade better than her first attempt, but the Wolf's Glen and Samiel himself still wouldn't scare the shit out of a living soul.

'Perhaps what they need is a spot of colour,' I said.

'Okay,' Norman replied without enthusiasm. 'We can get Hildie to do one spread in colour.'

'By the way, I've got this idea for a book about two American palaeontologists - '

'C-can it wait till later.' Norman was dressed in his dark chocolate brown suit with matching beige shirt and tie. Aftershave, brilliantine and smoker's toothpaste contested the air about him. One day each month he attended a board meeting at the offices of the parent company, just off Grosvenor Street, then lunch with Sarah at a nearby hotel, and a bit of this and that.

For the meeting he also had on his desk running sheets of *The Zany Zoo Book*, very large and thick coated sheets of paper, that kept rolling up when you tried to spread them out and added a strong whiff of printing ink to the brew.

'J-just what was needed,' Norman said on a happier note. 'A stronger story line and a b-bit more zip!'

At my suggestion, Croc the Doc, now in surgeon's dark-green garb, brandished a chain saw as he stood over a terrified patient strapped to the operating table. Penguin Pete, meanwhile, was supposed to be whacking the Wicked Weazel, with his bundle of swag, over the head with his truncheon. But he couldn't do it holding his truncheon right down there, where Hildie had put it. What the hell was she thinking of.

I got up and went round to Norman's side of the desk.

'Er, shouldn't Penguin Pete be holding his truncheon above his head?'

Norman suddenly blanched, and so did his rubber plant.

'Christ!' He nicked his finger on the sharp edge of the running sheet. 'Sarah!' He sucked at his finger. 'Cyril!' He lunged for his pack of cigarettes. 'H-Hildie!!'

*

Mind the gap! Another voice cried and cried out again in the Hades of the Underground. This time it was Blackfriars station on the Circle Line.

Yes, the trains went round and round, but they did not travel in anything like a circle. The route they followed was closer to the outline of a great sperm whale, with his massive head and abdomen swinging from Sloane Square round to Edgware Road, while his tail twisted from Liverpool Street to Tower Hill, which would just about place his anus at Blackfriars. And the old Fleet River, an open sewer for a thousand years, could not be better placed to serve his needs.

The Fleet River, from Anglo-Saxon times and for centuries to come, had carried the stinking detritus of the city into the already polluted Thames. It had long since been sanitised and hidden beneath New Bridge Street, where at low tide it trickled harmlessly and discreetly into the Thames beneath Blackfriars Bridge, while the sewage went elsewhere.

Talking of which, take a piss, have a crap, throw up, flush the toilet, out of sight out of mind, but never far beneath our feet, the huge torrents, rivers, oceans of raw sewage forever trickling, gurgling, gushing their way through the labyrinth of sewers and drains, conduits and pipes, uphill, down dale, on their tortuous way to the kind of treatment centres we also didn't care to know about. One day the pavements and roadways and buildings might collapse into that labyrinth of filth, to drown us in our own contagion.

Christmas coming up again, and as good a time as any, the parties, the piss-ups, swelling the flow till the sewers could take no more. Meantime, up above, the spirit of the season was already in the air. A red neon sign in an office window, flashing Merry Christmas over the green outline of a make-believe fir tree, blinked through the murk that hung about Queen Victoria Street. By Ludgate Hill it had condensed into a fine drizzle, turning patches of oil on the road into anaemic rainbows and trickling down the drains with the fag ends of life.

*

It wasn't just what went down the drains. After a couple of days the bins at the back of Linden Court were full to overflowing with our domestic waste. Multiply that kind of waste by God knows how many times to get some idea of what we all produced, the empty cans, the glass bottles and the plastic ones, the soiled paper and the cardboard, more plastic bags and wrapping, the greasy detritus of a million meals, the rotting food, the kipper bones, the lot. An Everest of it every day to dispose of, much of it dumped in those huge landfill sites, there to rot and fester and one day to erupt like huge terrestrial boils to choke us in clouds of toxic gas.

'Good morning, sir.' Through the big swing doors of The Central Criminal Court I was greeted by an officer in smart white shirt and tie. No Penguin Pete was he. 'First day juror?' He directed me to the cloakroom. 'You want Number Three Court.'

Two female officers also hovered close by, a blonde and a brunette, incarnations of those two enticing witches on Adrian's card, now dressed in constabulary garb. What was it about women in uniform that turned men on? Perhaps it was the thrill, real or imagined, of seeing in a woman something of themselves, a blurring of the sexual lines of engagement, with every fantasy that went with it. And, looking at those two feisty young officers, did it turn them on as well? The hair, cut short or brushed back into a bun, the white starched blouses over their boobs, tight black skirts and stockings, made all the more exciting by the air of authority and constraint. Try something on, they seemed to say, and feel us, smell us, as we take you down.

I'd try something on. 'Can you,' I asked one of them, 'direct me to Number Three Court?'

'Number Three Court, sir? Up the stairs, left at the top, then through the double doors,' she replied, with a chirpy smile reserved for the harmless likes of me.

*

The Old Bailey, I could tell Phyllis, to rub in her jealousy, takes its popular name from the adjoining street, 'bailey' meaning a fortified wall, maybe a Roman one. The original building stands on the site of the old Newgate prison, a solid tribute to Edwardian architecture and high-morality, topped by a handsome dome and a gilded though not blindfolded figure of justice, sword in one hand, scales in the other. The newer, much more workaday extension, appears from the street to have been stuck on. Inside it's a very different matter. To pass through those double doors, from new back to old, was to pass through a time warp, from a world of newly polished marble, perspex and foam rubber to one of Elgarian majesty and gloom.

The leaded tracery within those great big windows flanking the white stone staircase indicated stained glass, flat and colourless against the grey wet world outside. What light there was brought a faint answering gleam from the marble pillars and caught the particles of dust, held in timeless suspension.

There were already a number of other first day jurors assembled outside Number Three Court, sitting on the cracked leather and horsehair seats, or standing by them, silent and humble. It was like the first day at school or any other institution, you knew nothing, you were intimidated. A quote from the Bible seemed apposite. Like a sheep before his shearer is dumb. That was us.

One of our company, a woman, began to take off her coat, very slowly, button by button, one sleeve and then the other, pretty much like somebody trying self-consciously to unwrap a sweet at a concert or a play. For Christ's sake get on with it. She dropped her handbag, and it was a bomb going off.

That was just before the doors of Number Three Court burst open, disgorging a crowd, or rabble, of lawyers, policemen and other assorted types, all in a state of high excitement. Then, like a phantasmagoria, they evaporated into thin air, and the silence was heavier than before.

It was next broken by a rapid click of heels across the floor. A rather stout and fussy lady, in a gown but no wig, a sort of judicial sergeant major, trotted towards us. She held a clipboard and pencil.

'Right.' She called out our names and we answered with a nod, a grunt, a cough, a shuffle, the sheepish raising of a hand. She smiled briefly and beckoned. 'Walkies,' she said, and like poodles we obeyed.

*

'Do you think it was because of Penguin Pete's big stick that we all got shot?'

'You mean fired, Hildie. And I don't think Penguin Pete's truncheon had anything to do with it. I mean, the book's come out, hasn't it. In any case we weren't fired or given the push. We were made redundant. Taken over by a larger company, swallowed up by a much bigger fish, thrown on the scrap heap. It happens all the time. We're just pawns in the game of big business.'

'Porn?'

'Eh?'

'Like in dirty books?'

'No, pawns, Hildie. P-a-w-n-s. Pieces in the game of chess. They're like the infantry. Cannon fodder. Expendable. Not worth much. It's Cyril I feel really sorry for. He won't get another job at his age.'

'Ja, and it was Cyril who told me to put the stick down there.'

'I had an idea it might have been him. Like making a rude sign with his finger. He must have hated the way I sort of took over *The Zany Zoo Book*, though I didn't mean to hurt him. Ah, what the hell. We've got our names in print. We're famous!'

We sat before a very large painting in a huge gilded frame that must have weighed half a ton. The painting itself depicted a naval engagement, during the wars between the English and the Dutch to judge by the ships and the flags. The English warships had such names as 'Glorious' and 'Invincible', though they didn't look it in the heat of battle. Cannons roared at point blank range, sails were ripped to shreds, masts were broken off, and the water round the ships was red with blood, where men also clung to floating spars or drowned. There was, at the same time, a marvellous freshness to the brushwork, especially round the edges of the picture, the choppy sea, the play of sunlight, evoking the feel and tang of a good stiff breeze sweeping up the Channel or off the Naze. How many times had I seen it and breathed it just like that, off the end of the Palace Pier.

'How is it in the court?' Hildie asked next.

'I haven't started yet. It's not just one courtroom at the Old Bailey, there's fifteen or more of them, and they need a big pool of jurors just waiting around till they're needed.'

Hildie frowned. 'A pool. You are not swimming, I think.'

'No Hildie, we're not swimming, just sitting there like we are now. Shall we move on?'

I got to my feet, pressed my hands into the small of my back, and slowly stood up straight. Going round an art gallery or a museum, not walking but shuffling along, starting and stopping, bombarding the eyes with hundreds of impressions, soon did for both body and mind.

The only sensible thing was to concentrate on just one or two pictures or know in advance what you wanted to see and go for it. So, leaving the picture of maritime carnage behind, we drifted past rooms filled with cool Dutch interiors, vivid portraits of the old Spanish court with their dwarfs and dogs, vibrant French landscapes.

'Don't you think, Hildie, that art galleries are somehow all wrong? All these great paintings herded together in this artificial atmosphere, kept almost like pampered pets, removed from the real world. They should each have a special place of their own, in a church or in the room of a house or palace where they become a part of their surroundings. All crowded together like this, if you're not careful you just come away boggle-eyed.'

'Ja, I think that also.'

'Of course, the other thing about paintings is that there's only one original. Not like a piece of music or a book which is out there all the time. That's why paintings fetch these crazy prices at auctions. They're used like currency. Someone can buy a great painting for some huge sum of money, then lock it away in a bank vault so that no one else sees it for years and years. Absolutely scandalous.'

'Oh sure.'

'That's not all, or rather there's another side to a place like this. Look at all these great paintings. Think of the effort and experience and huge talent that went into each one of them. Then think of all the thousands of other paintings in galleries and museums around the world. All that achievement. It's like a crushing weight on top of you. The same with books. Go into any big bookshop or library. All the famous novels, the books of philosophy and science, all the poetry, all the plays. It's so hopelessly overwhelming. I mean, Hildie, what hope is there for us?'

'You can hope maybe. Not me.'

'Oh come on, Hildie. Forget everything I just said. Shake your fist at Rembrandt and say, I'll show you one day!'

At least that made her smile, as we entered a room where the light seemed suddenly to dim. In one painting a bloodless Saint Sebastian was tied to a post and pierced by arrows. In another there was Saint Jerome on his knees before a crucifix, mortifying himself by hacking at his breast with a sharp stone. Painted in dark colours on a panel of wood, yet another saint carried on his back the large iron grid on which he was shortly to be roasted alive, the manic gleam of martyrdom already in his eyes. And I think the women could be even more fanatical than the men. I recalled the story of one female saint who put her eyes out because she didn't feel worthy to look upon the face of God, so God put her eyes back, and she gouged them out again. I don't know who won in the end. And to mortify her flesh I think there was another lady saint who drank a bowl of blood and puss.

'There you are Hildie. See what religion can do for you.'

*

Saint George came as light relief, as depicted by Uccello. There he was, on horseback and in shining armour, meeting up with his legendary dragon. It was, in fact, the latter who grabbed your attention, an extraordinary beast on two legs, like a kind of mutated ostrich, with a long curly tail, and two huge bat-like wings. The other extraordinary thing was that he was held on a flimsy kind of chain by a chaste medieval lady, and he appeared to offer no resistance as Saint George poked out one of his eyes with a lance. With its bright, almost garish colours, the whole scene had a fairground gaiety.

'I feel sorry for the poor old dragon,' I said.

'Ja, me too.'

'Actually I think Uccello must have had a lot of fun painting this picture. Fine art doesn't have to be serious and saints don't have to be martyrs. I also wonder if there's a hidden meaning behind it, like there was to so many paintings of that period. An allegory.'

'How is that?'

'Well, perhaps Uccello was using the story of Saint George and the Dragon to say that he had a rival in love. The medieval lady was the object of his affections and the dragon was his rival.' I shook my head. 'A bit too obvious perhaps.'

On an impulse Hildie grasped my hand. 'Ja, and I think maybe you also have a story to tell with this picture. I think it means something special to you. I think you have a lot of things that make you unhappy that you don't want to talk about. Perhaps it is to do with when you were in hospital and perhaps you think that coming to see this picture with me might make you get rid of some kind of - .' Hildie let go of my hand. 'I don't know. I think I talk too much.'

I opened my mouth and closed it. I'll bet she'd never said so much in one go in her life. But she'd hit the nail on the head, or as near as damn it.

'Listen Hildie, perhaps one day - .' Another few words left hanging in the air. Incidentally, wasn't 'uccello' also the Italian word for 'bird'? Wheels within wheels. 'Come on, time we had a drink.'

*

Through the big plate glass windows of the jurors' canteen, the graphite-grey dome of St Paul's loomed above the rooftop clutter of old chimney pots, skylights, extractor fans and air ducts crawling python-like over brick and bitumen. The dome hid from view a large segment of the sky. Unlikely perhaps but not impossible that at that very moment the Second Coming had parted the clouds on the far side of it, and the golden cross atop the dome was about to blaze with reflected glory. Or perhaps it just hid the same porridge-grey mass of cloud hanging over Bermondsey and Blackheath. The point was, you never knew for sure.

That was the lure of all tall buildings, of hills and mountains, islands rising from the water, banks of cloud, even clumps of trees, or the moon waxing large and low on the horizon. What lay beyond and on the other side, beckoning the mind and the imagination? The rest of the universe in one way or another, going on and on, in a vortex of space and time, like a spiral, in the end was its beginning, so that it finally came round again to disappear up your own backside.

There was a sudden rush of activity in the canteen as a serving jury came in for a break. They clattered their trays and sat down in small huddled groups, sipping their coffee, munching on their buns and rolls, with an appetite born of those with a job to do. And while they chatted busily among themselves they were also aware of those of us just waiting to be called, casting quick glances in our direction, as much as to say, they knew the ropes. Then they glanced at their watches, got up with a noisy scraping of chairs, ready to return to the stews of justice.

Bugger them, my tooth was playing up again, what with all that canteen coffee, tasting more and more like mud, and those sausage rolls, all flake and very little sausage, the dregs of the catering industry.

In truth, it wasn't the tooth it was the gum. Inspecting it in the washroom mirror, I prodded the infected area and watched the blood rush back into the seat of it, or wherever the seat of it was. Difficult or impossible to identify the source or centre of any disturbance, in my gum or anything else. Watch the frantic activity if you disturbed a large ants' nest, or the awesome gathering of cloud in a thunderstorm, and try to pinpoint the centre of it all. I suppose what we were watching was matter, of one sort or another, trying to sort itself out and return to a state of equilibrium, although didn't something called entropy suggest that in the universe as a whole the reverse was going on, that the tendency was from order to chaos?

Ouch! Just leave that bloody tooth alone. It was already working loose. That was the next thing. 'Open wide', tug, crunch, the clatter of it on the dentist's plate and the tongue drawn irresistibly towards the sticky gap. Mind the gap.

*

Now that I had some experience of them I could speak with authority. 'Canteens are all the same, aren't they,' I said to Phyllis as cheerfully as I could. 'All smell of yesterday's custard.'

A plastic orange lay becalmed in a glass tank of the same coloured liquid, on top of the soft drinks dispenser. On the wall behind it the chuckle on the celluloid face of Father Christmas had slipped into a leer.

'I didn't know you smoked,' I said next.

'If you can't beat 'em, join 'em.' Phyllis puffed defiantly away inside a shaggy greyish-brown pullover, several sizes too big, unless she had shrunk still further.

'But this is a hospital.'

'This part's the funny farm.' She tried a funny face, which made things worse. 'They don't care.'

The fog of cigarette smoke in the room began to sting my eyes and throat. I'd also stink of it for a week, that and yesterday's custard.

'So why didn't you say?'

'Say what?'

'Where you'd gone.'

You can never tell with people. I'd have thought I was the only friend Phyllis had, but it was someone else in the block who told me she'd gone into hospital.

'Anyway, how are you?'

'How do I look?'

'Not too bad.'

'Liar!'

166

Phyllis still looked better than some of the other patients in the Recreation Room. Huddled together with their pinched grey faces and greasy hair they looked more like junkies.

I said, 'Some of the people in here look more like junkies.'

'They are junkies. The police take 'em off the streets and dump 'em here. We're all doped up anyway. It's the only way they can manage. Turn us into zombies.'

'But don't you see a doctor, a shrink, I mean a psychiatrist?'

Phyllis puffed out more smoke and emitted one of her little bird-like shrieks. 'They're all bonkers too!'

Ted's words came back to me. It takes a nut to cure a nut. A rather scary feeling was coming over me as well. Maybe this place wasn't quite Bedlam, but if you were as doped up as Phyllis suggested, how would you ever have the strength of will or the wit to get out of it again? And supposing they mistook me for one of the patients and gave me a quick jab too. I'd once struggled to understand Kafka but now I think I knew where he was coming from.

'Can I do anything for you? Get you anything?'

'A bottle of gin.'

'Gin!' Now we were back in the world of Hogarth and of Bedlam.

To add to it, from one dim corner of the room a kind of Amazon emerged from the motley throng. She was dressed in a sort of smock. The plait had gone, the hair now raggedly snipped off around the ears. But a phantom paperweight came hurtling through the air.

'Well, look who's here!' she bawled, pointing a beefy arm at me. 'My little Casanova. Can't deliver though, can he!'

Phyllis whipped round. 'You shut your gob. He's a lovely man!'

'Fuck off you, or I'll come over there and - '

A nurse, I assume, was on her feet, then a couple of male attendants appeared, the men in the white coats at last. Ingrid had the strength of ten, till they got the needle in.

*

We'd been called to form a jury at last, and I waited my turn to be sworn in. I'd never taken an oath before, and my mind turned back to the Bible. As a child I started to have my doubts about angels and miracles. Why did they only feature in the Bible? Why didn't they appear or happen today? Could it be that they never existed or happened in the first place? The Bible was called The Word of God. But it must have been written by dozens of different people over hundreds, maybe thousands of years, each of them reflecting a different cultural and historical period, each with a different take on things, a different axe to grind. And much of what they wrote, as with just about every other chronicle, must also have been based on hearsay. So how much of the Bible was true and how much was wishful thinking, legend or myth? In which case, what was holy about it? And, if that's what I thought, rightly or wrongly, why should I take an oath upon it? I might as well swear by the Koran or the Upanishads.

As a matter of fact, didn't I have the right to refuse to take such an oath on the grounds of conscience? Good. For the first time in my life let me stand up for my rights, demonstrate my free will.

'Take the Book in your right hand,' said the Clerk of the Court, 'and repeat the words on the card.' The judge was watching and waiting. Next time.

*

168

As chance would have it, we were back in Number Three Court, one of the original four, and it couldn't have changed all that much in close on a hundred years. Heavy oak panelling rose to a crescendo in the coat of arms above the judge's dais, while the dock was surrounded by iron spikes. Doctor Crippen, blinking mildly through his glasses, might well have stood or sat in that very one, guarded by a posse of policemen with mutton chop whiskers, tunics buttoned up to the chin and hobnailed boots. Perhaps the same ones who a few years before had patrolled the fog-bound, gas-lit streets of Whitechapel with their capes and great big lamps and their whistles, in pursuit of Jack the Ripper.

Romance was one thing, reality was another. The jury box was exactly what it said. It was a wooden box in which twelve good men and true, products of a more heroic age, would have thought nothing of sitting bolt upright for hours on end with the thinnest strip of padding for their backsides. Nor would such sturdy yeomen have been bothered by such things as pins and needles or the cramps. I slowly shifted a foot on the floorboards to try and relieve both, hoping that the lady seated next to me didn't get any wrong ideas. That was something you wouldn't have seen either. A woman in the jurors' box. Clear the court!

'Ladies and gentlemen of the jury.' Counsel for the Prosecution was surprisingly quick on his feet. He and that courtroom were a pair. Even in such a conservative world as the Law, with all its wigs and finery and arcane observances, there couldn't be many left like him. From a lifetime of familiarity, his own grey dusty wig sat upon his cranium slightly askew. He pulled his gown about him and toyed with a pendant on his watch chain that straddled an ample midriff. Wasn't there some fictional lawyer called Rumpole of the Bailey, who spent his life bowing to the judge and muttering 'M'Lud', when he wasn't consuming steak and kidney pudding, stilton cheese and port wine? Well, there he was made flesh, addressing us.

'Ladies and gentlemen of the jury.' Counsel's plummy voice went with the rest of him. 'It is the Crown's intention to prove to you, beyond a reasonable doubt.' And we were off.

*

Life in Linden Court wasn't the same without Phyllis. Take the post. When the rest of us had trotted off to work there was often no one else around to answer the postman and let him into the building, in which case he just shoved the mail through the downstairs front door letter box, where it lay scattered over the floor till we picked our way through it. And if he had a parcel that was too big for the letter box he left a note and we had to go and collect it at the nearest sorting office.

The writing on the package I'd just collected was large and loopy, like floppily tied shoe laces. It needed pulling together into a strong, tight knot. The parcel was from Hildie.

'It is crazy I know,' she wrote in the same large and loopy hand, 'but I hope you will like it better than Max and his Magic Shots.'

She had sent me a painting, this one done in oils on a small panel of wood. It portrayed two mounted warriors, one of them attired in red and gold pantaloons with a chain mail helmet topped by a plume and wielding a scimitar, the other with a turban wrapped round his head, and aiming a pistol at his adversary. Their caparisoned horses, a russet and a blue one, pranced over a stubbly field beneath a thick and turgid sky.

Hildie said she had copied it from another picture when she was still a girl. She'd done a lot more than that. It was primitive, wild, surreal, and you'd never guess in a million years that it was done by the same person who worked for Whizz Kid Books. It spoke of a talent and a vision found and lost again. It explained the way she scattered those pencil sketches for The Wolf's Glen and Samiel with her bare feet, the tears of frustration and anger welling up in her eyes.

'I have gone back home,' she continued, 'because my mother is now so ill, and I think I must be with her. I am sorry I did not have time to tell you, but perhaps it is better this way.' Perhaps it was. She hadn't quite finished either. 'I wonder why I think that deep down you are so unhappy. Perhaps one day you will come and tell me. Amsterdam is not so far. I am sorry. Maybe I talk nonsense. For this time, Happy Christmas, my darling man, from Mengelberg also.'

*

Hildie supposed that I was unhappy and in the very next breath she wished me a happy Christmas. Which was it to be? At Women's Fellowship, as well as fishing for men, they sang another chorus that spelt out, letter by letter, I'm H-A-P-P-Y. It continued, I'm sure I am, I know I am, as though they still had doubts. As well they might. We all knew about anger, sorrow, fear, regret, shame, and just occasionally joy and laughter. But happiness? A state of being so vague, when you stopped to think about it, as to be almost meaningless. Take us in that courtroom. The defendants didn't look noticeably unhappy because of their present predicament. And were we so happy as jurors because it was them and not us in the dock?

The second hand of the clock on the front of the public gallery ticked insistently away, and the light over the courtroom door flickered and softly buzzed, like Jock's old electric fire.

171

There were worse places to be in the depths of winter, nice and warm and something going on. But who'd want to be stuck in that courtroom through long hot summer days, and not even a window to open. No wonder they all looked so pale, those legal types. If they weren't in court they were back in their gloomy chambers buried in mountains of affidavits.

And why the wigs? They must date from the late seventeenth or eighteenth centuries, when everybody of any consequence wore a wig. In many cases it was because they shaved off their hair to be rid of fleas and mites. There was a portrait of Handel with his shaven head. He looked a different person without his wig. The point was, what made lawyers cling to their wigs when the rest of the world moved on? A black gown might lend them a certain gravitas. A wig was comic.

'May I now draw your attention to Exhibit Number Five,' Counsel for the Prosecution said in his plum pudding voice. We blinked at a set of glossy black and white prints, at a row of garages covered with obscene graffiti, at a smashed and abandoned car with fragments of broken windscreen strewn like diamonds across a lonely cul-de-sac, at a stretch of wasteland and some rusting railway tracks. Snapshots of a real and a desolate world somewhere out there that seemed to have nothing to do with us.

Closeted in our small oak-panelled courtroom, heads of the defendants ranged along the front of the dock like targets in a shooting gallery, counsel bobbing up and down, the judge wrapped in his crimson robe, taking the occasional note, glancing at the clock, the twelve of us packed like proverbial sardines in our box, we might all have been one of those old mechanical tableaux on the Palace Pier, consigned to a dusty corner away from the flash and clatter of the pin tables, while under the floorboards the grey-green waves sucked and gurgled round barnacle-encrusted stanchions and broke like thunder upon the shingle beach.

Somewhere below us came a faint rumble of the Central Line.

*

Back from the dentist my jaw dropped for a second time. There, at the top of the stairs, was Phyllis.

'They've let you out!' I cried, which wasn't perhaps the warmest or the most tactful welcome home. But after everything Phyllis herself had said about being doped up and detained almost under lock and key, I was surprised to see her at all. And what did she look like. The nightie, the Minnie Mouse pink slippers were the same, but the hair was all tangled up and crowned by a sprig of holly. She had a mug of something in one hand, and my post in the other.

She offered me the mug instead of the post. 'Have a drink,' she drawled. It looked like floor polish and was probably sweet sherry.

'No thanks, Phyllis, mustn't drink or eat anything for a couple of hours.'

She took a slurp from the mug. 'You're talking funny.'

'Just had a tooth out.'

'Oh, me Gawd!' Phyllis fell back against the wall. 'Listen.' She wagged a finger. 'I told her, didn't I. Told her to shut her gob. He's a lovely man, I said.' Phyllis took another slurp. 'Listen, why did she call you Cosa - ?'

'Cosa Nostra?'

'No!'

'Casanova.'

'Like I said.'

'Haven't a clue.'

Phyllis pushed herself away from the wall, took a couple of steps forward and flung wide her arms, spilling some of the contents of the mug, where it stuck to the floor.

'Are you,' I asked, backing off, 'still on medication?'

'When I want. Now come 'ere, Casanova, and give us a kiss!' She stuck out her tongue.

I snatched the post from her other hand. 'Got to lie down, Phyllis.'

'That's right,' she shouted as I very hurriedly closed my door behind me, 'you go and lie down. On your own, like me. Always on my fucking own, I am!'

*

Poor Phyllis, another stab of guilt, quickly cancelled by the indescribably appalling thought of her tongue, tainted with sweet sherry, reaching for the sticky blood clot where my tooth had been. I really did have to lie down fast.

When I felt a bit better I opened the post. A few more Christmas cards. Mum's was a card from a charity for the disabled, and made by them as well, by cutting out the picture from an old card and sticking it on a new one. It was a Nativity scene, stuck on not quite straight. A mawkish looking cow and a donkey peered into the crib. Hang on. Did they have any cows in the ancient Middle East? Not speckled ones anyway. 'Give my love to Ann,' mum wrote.

On a second card, healthily pagan, a robin perched on a snowy yule log. It was from Iris. She'd chucked her job, sold the house and gone to Norfolk to look after her bedridden mother. She and Hildie both. And was it a gender thing? The mothering instinct turned in upon itself.

'Mud everywhere,' Iris complained, 'and the whole place stinks of pigs.' So would we if we had to live like them.

'I'm writing a novel,' she went on. 'Giles...' Her writing trailed away up the side of the card, illegible. And not a word about Adrian.

From the other side of my door came a raucous snatch of song. 'I've Gotta Luverly Bunch of Coconuts!'

Dream on, Phyllis. Dream on.

*

The secrets of the jury room were embalmed in a yellowish film of tar and nicotine, walls, ceiling, lights, everything, from the days when smoking was a part of life. There were also cigarette burns on the massive old table, around which no two chairs were alike. A cast-iron radiator intermittently cracked with a bone-dry heat that made your bogeys rattle. Someone went to the toilet and there came the clank and gush of a chain and cistern that were a salute to Mr Thomas Crapper.

Through the window a white-tiled chasm led down to the cells, and on the other side of it brightly lit offices were festooned with paper chains and bedecked with jolly cards. They sat there all year round, eyeball to eyeball, giggling and gossiping, filing and painting their nails, then handed each other Christmas cards. Perhaps I was better off in the waiting room to nowhere.

'Right.' We took seats round the table in no particular order, till one of the ladies proposed as our chairman the gentleman with the short back and sides, the clipped moustache and regimental tie who also walked with a limp. An old war wound perhaps. He now took his place at the head of the table and we all shifted round.

He tapped his pencil upon solid wood and cleared his throat. 'Right. Shall we make a start?'

The bells of the City churches began to chime the hour, one after the other, as did the bells of Rome in the last act of *Tosca*. It was the sound of Christendom for over a thousand years, the great bells of the monasteries and cathedrals in their campaniles and their towers, ringing out over the olive groves and vineyards, mountains and hills, dark forests and sunny meadows, their myriad harmonics alternately clashing, corresponding, seeking a resolution in the Harmony of the Spheres. One very deep and sonorous bell, it must be from St Paul's, joined in, a mighty wave rising above the surging sea of tones and overtones.

The largest bell in the world, I recalled from *The Universal Encyclopaedia of Knowledge*, was in the Moscow Kremlin. Cast in bronze, gold and silver, and weighing over 200 tons, it stood on a plinth, where it dwarfed the visiting crowds, and with a great chunk broken out of it. This had happened during a fire and it had never been rung. If it had, and of that size, imagine its tone and its decibels, reaching out across the vast domains of Russia, from the Arctic to the Caucasus and way beyond the Urals, even ringing around the world, to set every other bell humming in sympathy until their collective vibration, huge and pulsating, would set the Earth itself throbbing and spinning out of its orbit and away towards the stars or into the sun.

'Hey you!' The chap across the table had a real strawberry hooter of a nose. I wanted to reach across and squeeze it like an old taxi horn. He glared at me and slapped his hand on the table. 'Are you in on this, or what?'

'I was thinking.'

'Well don't think too bloody long or we'll none of us be 'ome for bloody Christmas!'

Our chairman tapped his pencil on the table a little more severely. Ladies present, and all that.

*

Bells and terrestrial orbits aside, there was quite a lot else to think about if we put our minds to it. We had three defendants to consider, each on a different though related charge, and each represented by his or her own counsel. The virginal-white wigs of those defending counsel made a telling contrast with Rumpole's own grey, dusty and wise old head piece. The judge tried to compensate in his summing up but he still left me not much the wiser.

'Hey!' The Conk again. He and most of the others had their hands raised. 'What about you? Yes or no!'

'I'm abstaining.'

He again thumped his hands on the table in a gesture of exasperation. 'There's always one of 'em!' he cried.

Oh God, all right. I raised my hand in turn.

'That's better, my son!'

*

Trial by jury was sacrosanct. Was it connected with Magna Carta? At any rate, nobody questioned such a cornerstone of our constitution and our democracy. So how had it worked with us? There were the twelve of us, selected at random from the electoral register, bright or thick as two planks as the case may be, and with some knowledge of the law or none at all. The judge was there to give advice, but it was ultimately up to us to decide on someone's guilt or innocence. Had we done so correctly? And, by the way, why must it be twelve of us?

Wouldn't six serve just as well, saving everybody a lot of time and money?

Be all that as it may, we filed back into the jury box one last time. This then was the moment we'd all been waiting for, the dramatic and expectant hush as we delivered our verdicts, just as we'd witnessed it a hundred times on screen. We'd have had to wait a long time for that. In our absence a new bunch of lawyers had usurped the courtroom with their books and pink beribboned briefs, busying themselves for the next case. They waited in a totally disinterested way while our foreman gave our verdicts, and that was it.

I suddenly felt quite empty. For two weeks we'd all been bottled up in that small courtroom, judge, counsel, defendants, the twelve of us in our box, all trying to avoid eye contact, while some kind of a camaraderie had seemed to enfold us. There was even time for the occasional joke. In view of the season of the year, wouldn't it have been fitting for the judge, in wig and scarlet robe, to lead us in a farewell conga, round the courtroom, in and out of the dock.

Just thank you and goodbye.

*

Outside again in the street, it was too late for lunch and too early to go home. For anyone who cared to notice, the clear cold sky was turning from emerald green to indigo blue, with one very bright object, the planet Venus or perhaps it was Jupiter, over to the south east, roughly in the direction of Bethlehem. Closer to home, pools of vomit marked each dizzy step away from a pub, and a paper-hatted party spilled out of a restaurant doing a knees-up down the road. I stopped by a bookshop window piled high with Christmas bargains, that is, remaindered stock. It was somewhere warm to pass the time.

In through the door and a photograph of Sylvia Bloom grinned back at me from on top of a stack of hardback copies of *Know Your Aura*. Her own aura was conspicuously missing, but she'd had a perm, and wore a pearl necklace, and they'd toned down the beetroot complexion, though there was nothing to be done about those lips. Wasn't there some corny old gag? Your lips are like petals - bicycle pedals.

'Could I have your autograph, please?' I swung round and someone was fluttering her eyelashes at me.

God almighty. 'Penny!'

'That's right. I'm so glad you remembered.' She inclined her head. 'Fancy meeting you here.'

She spoke with exactly the same baby doll voice, half swallowing her words. The rest of her was horribly wrong, the perm (a more expensive one than Sylvia's), the dark blue jacket and skirt, the large black shiny handbag, the black shiny high-heeled shoes that made her a bit too tall. She might have been a minor royal come to snip a piece of ribbon. Not far off it, perhaps.

Penny held out a copy of *The Zany Zoo Book*, open at the title page. 'I knew you'd be famous one day! And it's so well written! What's it like to see your name in print?'

I struggled with my voice. 'All right.'

She inclined her head again. 'Hildegarde's a pretty name too. Do you know her well?'

'Fairly well.'

'And I love Croc the Doc, and Penguin Pete, though his truncheon looks a bit naughty in one of the pictures.'

'Yes, I know.'

She held out a gold pen. 'Just your name. No dedication. Much too sentimental.'

I laid *The Zany Zoo Book* on top of Sylvia Bloom and scribbled it on the title page.

'I didn't know you were left-handed.'

'Yes, a sinister type.'

'Not too much, I hope!' Penny inspected the signature at arm's length. Sinister, dexter, it looked like a confession signed on the rack. 'Thank you!'

I tried to clear my voice again. 'Listen, Penny - '

'Do you work round here?'

'No, I've just finished jury service.'

'Gosh, how thrilling! Or was it dreadfully sordid?'

'Neither really. Penny - '

'Weren't you going to write a book about music and the stars?'

'Music and magic.'

'That's right. Have you finished that too?'

'I gave it up.'

'Oh dear. How's Pistol?'

'Blunderbuss.'

'Yes, of course.'

'Penny, I never had a chance to thank you for Hieronymous.'

That stopped her in her tracks. She dropped the pen back into her handbag, then looked at me and then away. Was she about to cry? 'I hope,' she began, stopped, swallowed and started again in a rather unsteady voice. 'I hope you liked him.'

'He's the most precious thing I have.'

For a moment Penny stood there, back in her old skirt and blouse, hair falling about her face, the careless smudge of lipstick. She shivered, fumbled for the hankie in that bloody handbag, and made a big thing of blowing her nose. 'Good,' she choked, then straightened up and glanced at her jewelled wrist watch. 'Heavens, is that the time!'

'Penny, wait!'

'Must dash!' Just like someone else I used to know.

At the door of the shop, and clutching her copy of *The Zany Zoo Book*, she waved back with the tips of her fingers, stepped into a waiting taxi, and was gone.

*

No dedication. My mind started to race. What was that all about? To my darling Penny with all my love. Was that the kind of slush she was afraid of, in case someone, anyone else might see it too? And something else. Why was she buying *The Zany Zoo Book*? It didn't go with the rest of her. For a child, I supposed. Her child. Our child!! Don't even think of it.

I was cold and hungry and still half in shock myself, back on the platform at Blackfriars station. A train came in, and seated in the nearest compartment was a woman reading a magazine. She wore a fawn-coloured raincoat with a belt loosely knotted round the waist. But whatever she'd been wearing the figure underneath would still have come through for those who chose to see it. It was the way she held herself, the acute sense of self-awareness from tip to toe, legs crossed at knees and ankles but a million miles from Miss Perkins, relaxed and a trifle louche. And a mid-winter pastiness took nothing away from the lurking sensuality. Mind you, nurses, like lawyers, never saw much of the sun. They just knew every nook and cranny of either sex, they both served and dominated. On any other day she'd have let me take her, or she'd have taken me, every which way we wanted. What sort of idiot had left that morning without her phone number, even her address. A drunken one.

'Cathy!'

Stand clear of the closing doors. They slid together with a hiss and a thump, the train moved out, rear red lights retreating into the tunnel, disappearing round a curve in the track. How I let them slip through my fingers, or how I slipped through theirs.

*

'Magnum!' Adrian repeated. The way some things went around. He was back on the premises of Writer's Cramp, though it wasn't called that any more. Fags and Mags it proclaimed across the window of what was now, in effect, a large kiosk. The Fags spoke for themselves. The Mags were newspapers, magazines, chocolate bars, soft drinks, biros, pencils, sticky tape, razor blades, pipe cleaners, you name it. Adrian now rented the upstairs room, with a sofa bed, table and a couple of chairs, a lamp and a carpet that didn't make it to the skirting. He raised himself from his favourite position on the floor to grasp another litre bottle of Valpolicella.

'I'm not sure if this is a Magnum, but a large bottle anyway. Champagne,' I added, 'often comes in Magnums. But there are larger bottles than that. There's a Jeroboam and a Methuselah, and I think there's a real whopper called a Nebuchadnezzar.'

That brought a smile to his face. 'Nebuchadnezzar!'

I nodded. 'I wonder why wine bottles have got all these Biblical names.' As an afterthought I said, '*Nabucco* in Italian. An early opera by Verdi.'

Adrian grunted. 'Still on that music thing?'

'I told you, I gave it up.'

Outside, in the deepening gloom, a shroud of silence had settled upon the lighted streets and windows, not so much of peace and goodwill, as of exhaustion, of a final collapse among the dirty plates and glasses, the detritus of crackers, paper hats, streamers and nutshells and the Queen on the telly.

'I had a card from Iris,' I said.

'That's more than I did!'

'She told me she was writing a novel. I wonder how long that'll last.' I shifted in my chair. 'Christ, who the hell am I to talk! She also said something about Giles but I couldn't read the writing.'

'Living in a caravan, I believe.'

'Back to square one.'

'Back to square one.' Adrian waved an arm about his modest room. 'Like me.'

'What about the piano?'

He half sighed, half yawned. 'Sold it. Fetched a good price. Half the money's gone to Betty, of course.' He finished his yawn. 'You were married once, weren't you?'

'Yes.'

'What was her name?'

'Ann.'

'With all your women, never found anyone else?'

They don't come very often, those moments in conversation when you have the opportunity to drop all the pretence, the evasion, the shallow chit chat of everyday existence and reveal what really bugs you, the ball and chain of guilt, shame, regret, grief, desire, that you secretly drag through life. It must be like apologising, as I'd done to Phyllis, only much more so, a huge sense of relief, and of a kind of inner cleanliness, when you'd let it all hang out.

Penny, Hildie? A solitary aircraft drifted across the dark winter sky, navigation lights blinking. Five more minutes to Heathrow.

I reached for the bottle. 'No.'

*

Adrian stifled another yawn. 'Written anything else?'

Should I, shouldn't I tell him. 'A children's book with animals. Not zoology. Turning them into people, like a doctor, policeman, thief. What's it called when you give other creatures human forms and types? Anthropo- something.'

'I know what you mean.'

'Anyway, it's been published.'

'What's it called?'

'*The Zany Zoo Book*.'

Adrian laughed the way Penny had done when we talked about Ptolemy and Pythagoras getting pissed on cloudy nights when they couldn't gaze at the stars. Like the release of a huge and glorious fart.

'I thought that might amuse you.'

'I suppose that's when you were at, er -'

'Whizz Kid Books.' I held up a hand. 'I know. Have another one on me. But I'll tell you, writing for children isn't easy. You have to stop and think about every word and phrase. You have to put things as clearly and simply as possible, with no chance of a misunderstanding. It's a real discipline.'

Adrian nodded.

'I also wanted to write a series based on stories from music, well mostly operas and ballets. But that didn't get far before we folded.'

'The same old bloody story.'

'Yep, the same old bloody story. You get kicked in the balls at every turn. Just the same with another of my ideas for a children's book. 'Battle of the Bone Men'.

'What's that all about?'

'Sort of 'faction', historical fact tarted up a bit, all about two brilliant but crazy American palaeontologists, back in the nineteenth century, who raced around the old Wild West discovering all these huge fossil dinosaur bones, with the Indian Wars, the building of the railroads, going on around them. Dinosaurs and natural history, the Wild West, a bit of geography, all wrapped up in one. Large format with lots of colourful pictures.'

'Now that does sound good!'

'Smash hit, I'd say! But I've got nowhere with it. I've sent out a synopsis and specimen text to a dozen publishers and not one sodding nibble.'

Adrian sighed deeply. 'It's just as you said. Unless you're in the right place, or meet the right person at the right time - ' He didn't bother to finish.

'It's heartbreaking, that's all. It seems to me that in this life, this vale of bloody tears, you either settle for security, obscurity, the daily grind, or if you try to do something a little bit different, raise your head a couple of inches above the parapet, you're in for all kinds of grief.'

Adrian nodded again. 'By the way, have you heard about Brewster?'

'What about him?'

'Something in the newspapers, some scandal about him desecrating graves, down where he lives.'

'I don't believe it.'

'Remember what Sylvia Bloom said.'

'What did she say?'

185

'No smoke without fire.'

'That's what I said about your barbecue.'

'What?'

'Out in Iris's garden.'

'Oh God, yes.'

'By the way, I see she got her book out.'

'Who?'

'Sylvia Bloom. Our Daphne.'

'That's right.'

'*Know Your Aura*. I saw it in a bookshop. Bloody great pile of copies. Must have been remaindered.'

'Huh.'

'Her and Cindy, eh.'

'Don't start all that again.'

'How about the two of them up here now. A foursome.'

'More bilbos.'

'Dildos.'

'God.'

'Hand jobs too.'

'God!'

'And blow jobs.'

Adrian laid his head back on the floor, one hand lovingly clutching the bottle and with a seraphic smile on his face. 'Shouldn't they really be called suck jobs?'

'D'you know, Adrian, I never thought of that.' He was learning fast.

*

'Good to hear from you.' Kenneth could almost have been in the room and not the slightest bit fazed by my letter referring to what Adrian had said about dirty deeds in the cemetery. I could almost see him too, hammering away with two fingers at a typewriter that should have been Tiger Tank, then correcting his many typing errors in that spidery handwriting with its trail of blobs and blotches.

Yes, he wrote, there had been a spot of bother while he and Elizabeth were up in Scotland for the season. A bunch of crackpots had broken into the library, stolen some of his bits and pieces and started fooling about with them in the cemetery. Luckily someone spotted them and called the police. No harm done, though Elizabeth was a bit upset when the press got hold of it.

I couldn't see Kenneth in deer-stalker hat taking wild pot shots at defenceless stags and grouse. But I could not quite shake off the image of a moonless night in the cemetery, and of Kenneth armed with magic wand and book of talismans, accompanied by a small group of acolytes, gathered round the monkey puzzle tree. A soft prodding of spades into black earth, the dull knock of metal on wood and a laboured breathing as something heavy and awkward and slippery is lifted from its resting place. A whiff of corruption in the air. Kenneth stops to put a match to his pipe. Kerr-Booom! And the smoking shell of a homburg hat at the bottom of a hole in the ground.

*

Long before such goings-on, real or imagined, granny and I used to tend granddad's grave on Sunday mornings to the sound of the bells from St Mary's parish church. It was a full peel of eight bells, ringing the changes. What wonderfully arcane names they had too, those changing sequences of bells, little bob minors, grandsire triples and grandsire caters, tittums, keg megs, and weasels. They stood for the rhapsody of the

English shires, singing out over river and stream, meadows, woods and rolling hills.

Bell-ringing, or campanology, wasn't for the weak or the faint-hearted either. You practised first on hand bells, learning those changes from pages of directions that looked as fiendish as tables of logarithms, before you graduated to the belfry, where you then had to learn to time your pull on the rope to the answering chime. Back-breaking and thirsty work as well.

One bright Christmas morning my dad took me up the tower of St Mary's church to watch them at their task. From down below the bells rang joyfully upon the cold crisp air. Climbing the stone steps of the tower, the sound of them was muffled, gagged. Then through the door at the top, where the circle of bell-ringers bent, straightened up, hung on the ropes by the tips of their toes, in strange pantomime. Above the rafters they had unleashed a howling vortex of sound. My vocalising octopus, with whom they were playing a desperate game of tug of war.

*

'Take a seat.' My God, so it was Hugh, the very same, who had replied to my humble job application. And he'd hardly changed. The wax on his face may have lost a little of its shine. The combed-back hair may have loosened slightly from the scalp. That's all. The double-breasted suit and tie, the long grey socks and black laced shoes were exactly as I remembered them. I'd even bet on the suspenders.

'Take a seat.' Like Sylvia Bloom, he also affected not to recognise me. I must have changed compared with him, but surely not beyond recognition. Perhaps Hugh was just very shy. It hadn't stopped him from occupying that padded leather swivel chair behind the great big desk in the office with fitted carpets on the floor, framed art prints on the walls and lots of intimidating space. It would seem that there were two ways of getting to the top, or within spitting distance of it. You watched and listened and schemed and out manoeuvred your rivals by fair means or foul. Or you just beavered away, kept a low profile, did nothing to blot your copybook, and when the rest of them had shot each other down, there you were, right time, right place, ready, perhaps to your own surprise, to step up to the plate.

*

'Ah.' Hugh looked up with evident relief as his secretary came in with a tray bearing a tea pot, a dainty little jug of milk, a bowl of white sugar lumps, two cups, one for me, but a biscuit only for him.

Over his shoulder and through his big window the river was flowing fast upstream, muddy brown water flashing in the sunlight, flotsam bobbing and twisting in little waves and eddies.

That's what it was doing during the concert interval in the Royal Festival Hall. I might have been standing anywhere, looking across at the necklace of lights strung along the Victoria Embankment. So might she. These things just happen. She said, with a shy little glance, it looked as though the river was flowing the wrong way. I smiled and explained, that's because it was really an estuary as far inland as Teddington Lock, so it flowed in and out with the tides. Teddington, she volunteered, was where she lived, convenient for where she worked, at Heathrow.

So how about the concert? After the interval the programme included a Suite from the music Ravel wrote for the ballet *Daphnis et Chloe*. Perhaps the most ravishing orchestral music ever written, I said. Its opening was an evocation of sunrise. Plenty of other composers had been inspired by the idea of sunrise, but none could compare with Ravel's treatment of it. Picture a mythical Grecian landscape. Then the first ripple of sound on the woodwind and a slowly rising theme on the strings as the sky begins to brighten. The light grows gradually brighter and brighter till the sun finally rises above the horizon in a blaze of glory and with a shattering blaze of orchestral sound.

Back in the auditorium I sat in my seat thinking of her not very far away, sharing the performance with me and my heart ready to burst. We met afterwards and she just shook her head, simply beyond words, awestruck. We must meet again. She nodded. How about the National Gallery.

*

The honey-coloured voice, the honey-coloured hair, parted along the crown of the head and falling in a half curl round the nape of the neck, except when she was going on duty and she pulled it up into a bun. With that cute little hat perched on top, bright-eyed and bushy-tailed as she used to say, you'd never fly with any other airline.

'Your CV.' Hugh put a hand to his mouth and coughed. 'Your CV reads quite well.' He'd never been in love, or he wouldn't still look so unspoiled, so shiny and smooth. So was it better to have the shit kicked out of you, or just keep going through the motions, so to speak? All that madness, all that grief, when, as I'd said before, a few good bonks would have done the job.

Hugh gave his cup of tea the regulation stir. 'Tell me.' He examined his biscuit. 'What do you know about motor racing?'

I had a boss called MG, if that helped any.

(end)